ISBN 978-1-330-81208-2
PIBN 10108612

This book is a reproduction of an important historical work. Forgotten Books uses state-of-the-art technology to digitally reconstruct the work, preserving the original format whilst repairing imperfections present in the aged copy. In rare cases, an imperfection in the original, such as a blemish or missing page, may be replicated in our edition. We do, however, repair the vast majority of imperfections successfully; any imperfections that remain are intentionally left to preserve the state of such historical works.

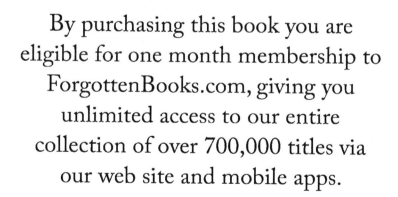

Similar Books Are Available from
www.forgottenbooks.com

Emma: A Novel, Vol. 1 of 3
by Jane Austen

A Tale of Two Cities
by Charles Dickens

The Jungle Book
by Rudyard Kipling

Neæra
A Tale of Ancient Rome, by John W. Graham

A Selection from the World's Greatest Short Stories
Illustrative of the History of Short Story Writing, by Sherwin Cody

And Quiet Flows the Don, Vol. 1 of 4
A Novel, by Mikhail Aleksandrovich Sholokhov

Les Misérables (The Wretched)
A Novel, by Victor Hugo

Agatha Webb
by Anna Katharine Green

The Alhambra
Tales and Sketches of the Moors and Spaniards, by Washington Irving

All Shakespeare's Tales
by Charles Lamb

Anna Karénina
by Leo Tolstoy

At the Foot of Sinai
by Georges Clemenceau

The Case of Mr. Lucraft, and Other Tales, Vol. 1
by Walter Besant

The Chartreuse of Parma
by Stendhal

Cheveley, Vol. 1 of 2
Or The Man of Honour, by Rosina Bulwer Lytton

Children of the Mist
by Eden Phillpotts

A Cornish Droll
A Novel, by Eden Phillpotts

Dark Hollow
by Anna Katharine Green

The Deaf Shoemaker
by Philip Barrett

Doctor Hathern's Daughters
A Story of Virginia, in Four Parts, by Mrs. Mary Jane Holmes

THE

STRIKE OF A SEX

A 𝔑𝔬𝔳𝔢𝔩.

BY

GEORGE NOYES ᵣMILLER,

(Member of the Oneida Community).

LONDON:

WM. REEVES: 183, CHARING CROSS RD. W.C.

Printed by the New Temple Press, Grant Road, Croydon.

SPECIAL PREFACE TO ENGLISH EDITION.

An English edition of this celebrated American story seems called for by the great and increasing interest felt in the problem of property in the old and crowded countries of Europe. It is nearly a hundred years since Malthus expounded the true relation between poverty and the increase of the human race : and it is more than thirty years since Darwin, in his "Origin of Species," showed that the Malthusian Law lies at the basis of all organic evolution. No further apology is needed for a tale which points to a discovery, already tested by experience, which claims to solve, at one and the same time, the Malthusian or population problem, the Darwinian or eugenic problem, the problem of social purity, and the problem of personal health in relation to sex.

F. W. F.

AUTHOR'S PREFACE.

To tell the truth, I put forth this slight piece of literature in much fear and trembling. Not that I had any morbid dread of literary condemnation, or any solicitude about financial failure. My anxiety was solely in regard to the reception that my little book might meet from women. To my mind, there was no other judge: and I awaited her verdict in real suspense.

But my suspense was happily short and in its relief, I think that I tasted something like the overpowering joy which the prisoner feels when he is declared to be innocent. The letters of gratitude which I have received and am receiving from noble women in two continents have fairly overwhelmed me and they have rewarded me a hundredfold.

The whole world is plainly in travail to lift the primeval curse of brutalizing labour from man. But the just, at least, are beginning to perceive that the primeval curse must also be lifted from woman. When these long-borne curses are really lifted from man and woman—what then?

The Garden of Eden!

GEORGE NOYES MILLER.

188, WEST HOUSTON ST, N.Y.
JAN., 1891.

WOMAN'S FUTURE.

Oppression with her leaden mein
Nor there is seen,
Nor can the wrinkled brow of Care
Find entrance there.

THE STRIKE OF A SEX.

CHAPTER I.

I w ιs greatly fatigued, and a feeling of irresistible drowsiness had begun to creep over my senses, when my flagging energies were suddenly aroused by the appearance of a town which, though I had not before observed it, now seemed quite close at hand. Tall and graceful spires, glistening domes, and high-rearing chimneys, from which poured plentiful volumes of smoke, betokened a place of thrift and business importance. I therefore began to enter one of its residence streets with the pleasant mental ex-hilaration which the pedestrian feels when he opens his eyes and ears to the sights and sounds of a strange city.

But I had not gone far before I was compelled to

acknowledge to myself that the city belied in some unaccountable respects the smart appearance which it had borne from a distance. The men whom I began to meet, although seemingly full of a kind of jaded activity, bore strange marks of carelessness, not to say positive disorder in their attire. Their untrimmed beards showed a great lack of taste and neatness. Their collars and cuffs were soiled and wrinkled, and their neckties, fastened about their necks in all sorts of ungainly knots, were very much awry. All had a deeply pre-occupied air, and I noticed that many of them had a finger or hand clumsily wrapped in rags of a mottled and dingy hue, as if they had met with untoward accidents, such as burns, cuts, or bruises. The odour of arnica pervaded the atmosphere.

But I soon began to perceive that the most perplexing feature of this universal disorder, or I might say dilapidation of attire, was the total absence of buttons from garments of every description. It was as if some greedy speculator or anaconda-like Trust had suddenly made a corner of the entire product of buttons and put them so far beyond the reach of his kind that man had been compelled to supply the place of these indispensable little articles with all sorts of mechanical makeshifts. Pins, strings, hooks, and I observed in some instances, shingle nails, held together the textile frame-work which invested every man I saw.

When I had become somewhat accustomed to this oddity, although inwardly much wondering what should cause it, I began to observe that the residences themselves although substantial in structure and ornamental in design, bore the same marks of surprising carelessness that I saw in their owners. The fine stone and marble doorsteps were strangely littered and untidy. Curious utensils for such places such as coffee-pots and dishpans, stood in the front windows of the various rooms. The parlours, which I could plainly see through the carelessly left open windows, were in a state of great disorder. Dust and confusion seemed to reign unmolested, and the curtains were clumsily fastened as if by unskilful hands.

These visible signs of a slatternly kind of housekeeping seemed to multiply as I advanced, but my attention to them soon began to be somewhat distracted by my sense of smell. Mysterious and inscrutable odours, defying all my powers of analysis, emanated from these residences. From one it was like burnt rags, from another it seemed to be grease in some stage of decomposition, from another the

odour·was that of musty and decaying food, while
from still others there proceeded an indescribable
mixture of all these.

More and more puzzled by the strange sights and
smells to which my senses had grown more acute as
I proceeded, I soon found that they were, after
all, almost wholly driven from my mind by an infinitely sharper sense of the utter joylessness of·the
place.   In spite of the hurrying crowds of men who
jostled one another upon the streets, I began to be
conscious of an overpowering sense of desolation
such as I had never before known.   An unaccountable gloom, which seemed to cover the whole town
like a funeral pall, began to settle upon my hitherto
buoyant spirits.   It was as if the sun were not
merely obscured by a passing cloud, but had been
wholly withdrawn from the heavens, leaving the earth
to be lighted only by some murky and baleful star.   I
recalled the fact that though many of the irregulari-
ties of apparel which I had noticed were in a high
degree ludicrous, I had not seen the ghost of a
smile upon the face or heard anything approaching
a jest from the lips of a human being since I entered
the town.   I attempted to arouse myself and shake
off the deadly chill that was beginning to envelope
me, and as I did so I unconsciously muttered, " One

would think it were the town of Hamelin from which the Pied Piper had just drawn away all the children."

No sooner had these words passed my lips than, like an electric shock, I remembered that I had not only not seen a child but I had not seen a woman since I entered the town. This dizzying fact was so astounding to me that I stopped in sheer and sudden fright and leaned against a tree near at hand in order to assure myself that it was true. Step by step, with minutest accuracy, I went over in my mind the ground which I had trodden. I recalled the anxious, hurrying figures of men, whose oddities of raiment no longer tempted me to smile, but not the face of a woman could I conjure up in the retro-spect, nor even the glimpse of a woman's garment. I had not, with a weakness which I think the angels forgive, turned on the streets to look after a woman's beautiful figure. I surely had not seen a woman on those unswept doorsteps, I had not caught a glimpse of a woman in those dust-ridden parlours. Even the blooming faces and joyous, sparkling chatter of school-girls had been wholly absent from the streets which I had traversed.

With a sigh I thought of the still younger girls, the unspeakably innocent little ones of three and four years of age whose charming prattle I tried to persuade myself that I had surely heard about some doorstep. But no, I never failed to notice these darlings, and my memory told me with unfailing accuracy that I had seen only men. Men, no one but men, bald, angular men, and these in their bold loneliness appearing to be robbed of all the graces and sweetness of immortal beings!

My speculations as to the meaning of the strange state of things which I had observed in the town into which I had fallen, had hitherto been only those prompted by a dignified and philosophical curiosity. But the shock which I experienced on discovering the utter absence of woman from my environment had now made them positively painful. I stood still and shivered in the street. Surely I had gotten into an uncanny place, from which the sweetness and beauty of woman and the innocence of children had been banished! I could bear the suspense no longer. Casting my hitherto dignified deportment to the winds I ran recklessly after a man who had emerged from a drug store at some distance in front of me and seized him almost rudely by the arm.

CHAPTER II.

It was a fine-looking man that I had thus unceremoniously grasped by the arm, albeit he seemed to be plunged into the same deep dejection that I had observed in all his fellows. Like them, his hair and beard were neglected and unkempt, and there was a devouring melancholy in his eyes. His collar, instead of being fastened by any mechanical contrivance, depended solely upon his scarf for being held in place. This scarf was closely tied around his neck in a hard knot. Occasionally, when he turned his head to one side or the other, one end of his collar would escape from the scarf and stand off from his throat at an obtuse angle. But of this he appeared to be quite careless, and for the most part unconscious. Like many other men whom I had seen, one hand was awkwardly wrapped up in a cloth of sombre hue, and in the other hand he carried a bottle labelled "For Burns."

"Excuse me, sir," I cried, "but I beg you to tell me what horrible misfortune has befallen this place. It seems like a land of mysterious mourning. Has some fearful plague devastated it? For Heaven's sake, tell me, where are the women?"

The man regarded me with an air of deep surprise, which, however, lent no animation to his cheerless countenance as he replied:

"Is it possible that you are not aware of the Great Woman's Strike which has now been in progress here for more than three months? The women of this country have combined as a sex to utterly refuse to perform any longer those duties and functions which have hitherto been magnanimously marked out for them by man as being the sole tasks pre-destined for them by the Creator. They say that the chains which have bound them for unnumbered ages, although artfully garlanded with flowers and called by sentimental and endearing names, are older and more galling than those of any bonds-people on the globe. They have decided that the time has come to throw off those chains."

"Do you really mean," I gasped, "that the women have struck for what they suppose to be their rights, *as a sex?*"

"That is exactly what I mean," replied the man,

" They have struck for their rights as a sex ; " and he fumbled for the end of his collar.

My surprise at this statement was so overwhelming, the idea of woman ever combining and striking as a sex had been so utterly undreamed of in my philosophy that I could not speak for several moments, seeing which the man said, while for the first time a sickly and self-conscious smile appeared upon his features:

" I must be off. I left my clothes boiling on the parlour stove this morning, and as it is now past noon, I fear that the water has all boiled away." And he turned away.

" But for God's sake," I cried after him, " where have the women gone, and their innocent children ? Tell me that before I flee from this accursed place and shake its dust from off my feet forever. Surely the women have not made away with themselves ? "

" Oh, no," said the man, " it is not quite so bad as that. The women have simply wholly withdrawn from their habitations with men. They have taken possession of the commodious buildings of a large institute on the hill overlooking the town. There they confer with delegations from the masculine authorities. They left not a single female of any class in the town, taking with them even the poor, the sick, and the aged. The grandmothers, the matrons, the blooming girls of sixteen, and the little girls of four or five are all together there. All male children who were so young as to be dependent on their mothers for care they also took. There is not a woman young or old in the town. Woman's abandonment of man has been complete, and," he added with a shudder, "final, unless the guarantee they ask is given them."

Having said this the man hastened down a side street, cutting, as I afterwards remembered, a very grotesque figure, the tails of his buttonless coat flying loosely behind him.

But the questions which now began to crowd my excited mind respecting the strange state of affairs by which I was surrounded, imperatively demanded an answer, and I lost no time in looking for some one who should further satisfy me. The man who first caught my attention was loitering near a corner, apparently studying the numerous advertisements of pain-killers, salves, ointments and cures for burns which were conspicuously displayed in the windows of a drug store. He stood with his hands in his pockets, and had a more jaunty air than any one whom I had yet observed. He was tall and thin, with whiskers on the end of his chin. There was a look of loquacity about him which encouraged approach, and also a "make the best of it " air which had the effect of somewhat relieving my painful concern of mind. This man had given up collars entirely. His coat was wide open and his whole attitude seemed to defiantly assert that collars and buttons were not, and never had been, any essential part of his make-up. To my observation respecting the Woman's Strike, which I made as general and incidental as possible in order to get at his view of it, he replied :

"Yaas, it's a kind of a hinderment. But the worst thing about it is the set-back it's going to give the population here in Hustleburg. Now there's Sprawltown, the rival town in our county what's trying to git the County Seat away from us. At the last census by doin' some of the tallest kind of lyin' and takin' names off from all the tombstones in the cemetery, they made out that they had about five more inhabitants than we had. Well, now to make things wuss, the women of Sprawltown didn't tumble to the idea of strikin' till about a month after the women of Hustleburg did, an' the birth rate goin' right on'll give it a great start.'

"Do you mean to say that the Strike has completely separated husbands and wives ?" I asked.

" Reckon it has, stranger," replied the man. "Oh a woman's got grit when she makes her mind up, and they say they're goin' to have their rights this time or they'll let the race die clean off from the globe. Shouldn't wonder, if this thing ain't settled before long, if some one should have the chance to act out the part of 'Campbell's Last Man' that I used to speak when I went to school. If I am the last man you can just bet I'll go over to Sprawltown to declaim it after every one there's been laid out. I'd just like to show that snipe that edits the *Sprawltown Git There* that the population of Hustleburg was ahead once without counting any dead men either."

" But how did the women get the idea of striking for their rights in this unheard of way ? Such an idea was never before to my knowledge discussed or dreamed of."

" Well," said the man, " that young fellow who is coming yonder can tell you a good deal more about it than I can. He was engaged to be married when the Strike came on, and what did his best girl do but drop her weddin'-dress, half finished as if it were a hot pertater, and leave him like a shot. Jehosophat ! to think that Solomon, the wisest man that ever lived, should ask thousands of years ago, if 'a bride could forget her attire,' and then to have one up and do it here in this nineteenth century. I'll introduce you to the young chap. He's naturally desperately anxious to get things fixed up, and he knows just what the women want."

The young man referred to, who had now come up to where we stood, was a broad-shouldered, good-looking young fellow who bore a serious, introspective air, together with one of brave manliness. My chance acquaintance introduced the young man to me as Mr. Justin Lister, and I offered my name in return—Rodney Carford.

I was impatient to begin serious conversation with Mr. Lister, but our loquacious introducer stopped long enough to say, as he pointed at the advertisements, in the druggist's window, of oil for burns, which were named after all the saints in the calendar :

" This man who runs this drug store's gettin' ready to retire from business. Got rich sellin' arnica and St. Huldy's oil since the strike began. You see men can't monkey around stoves and flat-irons and such things in a kitchen without knockin' the skin off from their knuckles and burnin' their fingers. They ain't got the patience of women, if they had the skill. I'm thinking of buyin' this man out if the

Strike continers, and as I know two or three other men who've got their eyes on the place, I'll have to leave you to close up the deal." And he disappeared into the drug store.

CHAPTER III.

I turned eagerly toward Mr. Justin Lister, as soon as our companion had left us. He was about my age, and there was a certain sympathetic friendliness in the glance of his frank blue eye that established a kind of magnetic rapport between us at once. It was therefore an easy matter for me to ask the privilege of accompanying him wherever he was going in order that I might have an opportunity to talk with him. He assented to my request readily and added that he was going to his own house, and if I could put up with such awkward hospitality as a man unassisted by woman could give, he would be pleased to entertain me. I accepted his offer with pleasure, and as we walked leisurely along the well-paved and shaded street, I lost no time in begging him to acquaint me with the beginning of this astounding Woman's Strike. " How did it come about ?"

"Why," said Mr. Lister, "it came about in the most simple way in the world, so simple in fact that it reminds one of Artemus Ward's story about the man who was confined for sixteen years in a loathsome dungeon without food or drink. A bright idea struck him and he opened the window and got out. You remember what an eye-opener the great Strike of the London dockmen was; the whole world suddenly realized, as by an electric shock, that Labour, instead of being the footstool or fawning slave of Capital as it had stupidly been assumed to be, was easily its master. Through its enormous power for combination, Labour was King, and could dictate terms to Capital which it could enforce whenever it pleased. This discovery, for it was as really a discovery as if a new continent had been found, illumined the whole civilised globe. All classes of people in the world who were suffering from oppression began to look carefully about them to see if the weapons for their deliverance were not lying unperceived and rusting in their own hands. Like a flash of lightning the women of this country saw that they possessed as great an advantage as the _ndon dockmen did. They saw that by combining as a sex into one solid mass they could place such limitations and embargoes upon man, as would wrest from him at one master-stroke the tardy rights for which they had been cringing and suing for wearisome years. Why, good Heavens! the very perpetuity of the race was in their hands. About this time also there was much earnest talk in many periodicals which sprang up, about the ' Brotherhood of Man.' Strange as it may appear, the women suddenly took up the notion that if all men were brothers, all women were none the less sisters, and as such should minister to each other like sisters, and protect each other from all harm. This great idea of the Sisterhood of Women, joined with woman's discovery of her real power when in combination, led to the Great Woman's Strike which you see now in progress."

" And this," I said, a sudden light breaking in upon my mind, " is, of course, the cause of the utter lack of taste and neatness which I see everywhere, in the persons of men as well as in the keeping of the dwellings. And can it also be the reason," I added musingly, " that I see no buttons on the garments of any one rich or poor ?"

" Oh, the buttons!" said Mr. Lister, with the first genuine laugh that I had heard that day; " one of the first things that the women did after the strike began, was to send word to the tailors, that inasmuch as the sewing of buttons on to garments had from time immemorial been the chief high prerogative which man had grandly conceded to woman, they did not propose to allow any one to take it from them. Small and poor as woman's privileges had been in the world's great history she could not part with a single one of them. They made the poor tailors quake in their shoes by threatening that they should never know the smile of a woman again if they sewed a single button on to a garment of any kind. The tailors hastened to send a delegation to the Women's Executive Committee, meekly promising to obey. They even offered to take the buttons off from all the garments they had on hand, if any such propitiation was needed."

" This regulation in regard to buttons, must have been rather hard on the button manufacturers ?" I suggested, with an effort at jocularity which I had not deemed possible under the circumstances.

"Yes," said Mr. Lister, "it has completely extinguished that industry for the present. I understand that the Button Manufacturers have a delegation now on its knees before the Woman's Executive Committee imploring them to rescue them from gaping ruin. But the young woman who is chairwoman of that committee is a person of great spirit, a regular Jeanne d'Arc. She will never yield," and Mr.

Justin Lister sighed so deeply that I suddenly remembered that the Strike had summarily deprived him of a prospective bride.

We walked along in silence for a few moments when all at once it occurred to my mind that I had not made any inquiry as to the nature of the rights for which woman was contending.

In fact, I had assumed, so completely as a matter of course, that the rights she was asking for were simply those which I had seen from time to time sarcastically enumerated in some scoffing newspaper, that it seemed unnecessary for me to say as I did to Mr. Lister :

" These rights which women are asking in such an imperious fashion are doubtless the old ones with which I am familiar : greater security in the holding of property, the right to vote, and to be eligible for all civil offices, including, perhaps, the Presidency, to be placed on an equal footing with man, as re- gards wages and all material advantages. These, doubtless cover all the things that they are con- tending for ?"

" Oh, no," said Mr. Lister, "every one of the things which you mention were granted to women within two weeks after the strike began. So far as they are concerned, woman is to-day the full equal of man.

Those rights were all included in one great Omnibus Bill, which was passed as quickly as the most expert legislation could accomplish it. I assure you that such was the awful completeness of the Great Woman's Strike that it did not take man three days to discover that life was not worth living without her. If it had been simply the withdrawal of a single class of women and their absence from a few scattered households the effect would not have been so absolutely terrifying. But to have woman forsake man as a whole, completely withdrawing her graces and softening in fluences from his environment, created a monstrous chasm, a void, at which angels might shudder. It was like the divorce of Heaven and Earth, or as if the lamp of civilization had suddenly been turned down, and men appeared to each other in the twilight which ensued like strange, wolfish animals."

"I can readily understand that," I said with a slight shudder, " but if all the rights I mentioned have been granted to woman, I cannot conceive of any further occasion for the Strike. Why is it not at an end ?"

"It is not at an end," said Mr. Lister, " because since woman has discovered her power, she has greatly enlarged the category of her rights, and it includes one now beside which all those you have named are trivial indeed. She has fitly named this great right her Magna Charta, nor could she have ever made such an unprecedented stand as she is now making on a less vital principal of justice than that of Habeas Corpus. It is a striking evidence of the tremendous attachment that exists between the sexes, that man, eager for the restoration of the cheering sunshine of his natural companion, was disposed to grant this final great concession as precipitately as he did the right to political equality, but it could not be done so lightly. It called for the most serious, philosophical consideration on the part of every individual man, and therefore some time has unavoidably elapsed. But the frightful contingency of allowing the race to lapse from the earth admits of but little delay. The granting of Woman's Magna Charta is to be decided by the ballot. To-day is Friday and on Monday next the fate of the world will be decided."

" What is this Magna Charta?" I said in awe, for the picture which my companion's words brought to my mind of a desolated planet reeling through space, made me feel strangely weak. I could scarcely persuade myself that I was not dreaming.

"The Woman's Magna Charta," replied Mr. Lister, " is—"

But at this moment a passing newsboy shouted, "Extra Hue and Cry! Rejection of the Button Manufacturers' Petition! Complete collapse of the Corset Industry! Great failures among the Ladies' Tailors!"

My friend bought a copy of the paper and leading the way up the steps of a handsome residence, at which we had now arrived, said:

"You are heartily welcome to my home, but I must again remind you that the soul of all delicate and artistic hospitality has vanished from it. It does not contain a woman."

CHAPTER IV.

Although the house to which Mr. Justin Lister now introduced me was more orderly than many which I had observed on the streets through which I had passed, the absence of woman from its walls was still painfully apparent. It was as if warmth and light and flowers and sweet perfumes were suddenly wanting in a place in which you had always been accustomed to find them and to solace yourself with them. Indeed, the suddenness of woman's flight, if I may so term it, was brought much more sharply to my consciousness by this visit to a house in which she had so recently held sway. There were unmistakable signs on every hand of unfinished feminine occupations. The piano stood open with a sonata by Beethoven lying upon it; artistic needle-work with the needles still sticking in it lay in a window seat, and a half finished sketch upon an easel all bore mute but telling testimony to the irreparable loss of gentle and artistic hands. Plants which had evidently had the cherishing care of feminine tenderness were languishing in a window, and a drooping canary disconsolately buried its head in its feathers in its cage. But that which weighed most heavily upon my sunken spirits was the indescribably pathetic sighing and whining of a large Newfoundland dog as he constantly roamed from room to room in search of a mistress's caressing hand. I finally had to entreat Mr. Lister with tears in my eyes to put him away where I could not see his grief.

Mr. Lister, as he explained to me, had lost not only his sweetheart and prospective bride by the Great Woman's Strike, but his mother and two sisters as well. This fact raised the question in my mind as to how the women were supported in their retirement, and I said:

"I can easily understand how the dockmen of London could stand the hunger of protracted idleness with their muscular frames and rude tastes, but how can refined and delicate women undergo the hardships of such a siege?"

"You forget," said Mr. Lister, "that the London dockmen had many sympathizers who contributed food and money to their cause. The women also have a legion of sympathizers, and if they had not, no man who has a mother or a sister would see them want. The result is that the women are like a vast army which is voluntarily supported by the very persons with whom they are in controversy."

The meal which Mr. Lister now prepared with his own hands, consisted wholly of canned meats and vegetables which he had procured from a neighbouring grocery. These he had warmed on the stove in their original packages, in order, as he explained, "to save dish-washing." "Fourier," he added, "was claimed by his disciples to be a truly great man, and in his 'Division of Labour' he did not put dish-washing into the 'Class of Attractiveness,' but into the 'Class of Necessity,' so you see I am trying to dispense with it altogether."

But the rudeness of the service or the incompleteness of the meal scarcely provoked a thought, so deeply was my mind engrossed by the consideration of the astounding facts of which I had that day for the first time been made aware. I had read and heard many times before, with a pang, of the breaking up of single households and the parting of husbands and wives by divorce, but to have the ties which bound together all men and all women sundered so suddenly, produced a groping confusion of mind that

made it impossible for me to think with any con-
tinuity. I mention this fact because it may seem
strange to the reader that I did not immediately
pursue my inquiry as to the specific nature of the
right which woman was asking of man. To tell the
truth, that inquiry had for the time being entirely
passed out of my mind, and I could only express such
fitful ideas as came to me without any premedita-
tion.

When the simple meal was finished and the cans
containing it were (manlike) tucked away in the corner of a bookshelf, we settled ourselves in easy
chairs for the evening, and Mr. Lister produced
cigars. After we had smoked for a few minutes in
silence, I said, as the first thought that chanced to
come into my mind:

"I understood you to say that the Strike included
all classes of women, but of course you excepted the
courtesans. I cannot help wondering how the Strike
affects their condition."

"Courtesans!" said Mr. Lister in a tone of deep
surprise. "Don't you know that there are no courtesans?"

"No courtesans!" I exclaimed. I abruptly arose
from my chair and walked aimlessly into the centre
of the room. Then, partly recovering myself, I walked

back and again sat down. The continuous suc-
cession of surprises which the day had brought to
me had insensibly worn upon my nervous system. I
repeated mechanically, more to myself than to Mr.
Lister, " No courtesans! "

" Yes," said Mr. Lister. " I did not think but
that you knew it, there are no courtesans. When
woman saw that the success of her movement depended upon her solidly combining into one vast
Sisterhood, she was confronted at the outset by the
fearful chasm which existed between her and her so-
called fallen sisters. How could the chasm be bridged?
Studying this problem with agonizing earnestness,
woman soon saw that the only way to solve it was
for woman herself to at once and forever abolish the
courtesan class. She clearly recognized the fact,
and it was like a revelation to her, that the courtesan
was but the extreme victim of an intolerably cruel
and satanic dispensation ; that the courtesan had
been but a little more deeply trodden under foot
than her more respectable sister. With this new
view woman utterly discarded the idea that the
courtesan was a special sinner to be approached with
a moral tract and a condescending kind of forgiveness. The courtesan had been unspeakably sinned
against, not only by man but by woman as well, and

more, perhaps, than any sufferer from cruelty on the globe, deserved the loving pity and succour of her sisters. Seeing this, with real contrition the women decided at once that it was their first business to take these sisters who had been so cruelly perverted by man, to their own bosoms, not as if they were prodigals, but as if they were loved ones who had met with the most cruel blow of misfortune.

This, bear in mind, was the first great act in the Woman's Strike. By an edict which was as effectual and will be as celebrated in history as Lincoln's Proclamation of Emancipation, woman has forever abolished the courtesan class. There can never be another courtesan, simply because woman has formed a self-protecting league that will never permit it. Dastards there may be among men who will hereafter seek to take advantage of woman's love, or her sweet complaisance toward man, but if such there be it were better for them if they had never been born. They only will be the sufferers. Held up to the scorn of the universe and forever ostracised by woman, their punishment will be as heavy as Cain's. But whatever may take place, woman will never again allow one of her own sex to lose caste through man's treachery. They will defend each other against the world."

. " Can it be possible," I said, "that so terrible a problem as the social evil, that has been hopelessly discussed by moral philosophers for ages, could be solved so quickly, and by woman, too ? "

" And who in God's name," said Mr. Lister, " if you stop to think of it, who but woman could ever abolish the courtesan class ? Certainly not man. He is constantly creating courtesans. Nothing but a self-protecting league among all women, uniting them into one common sisterhood, could ever have stopped this evil. Moreover, the power to do it came with their combination into a universal sisterhood."

Too much overwhelmed by the strange things that I had heard to keep up the conversation, I sank into a seemingly hopeless labyrinth of confusing thoughts. This lasted till Mr. Lister, who observed that I was very tired, showed me to my room, having first accomplished the somewhat difficult and precarious task of filling a lamp with coal oil. The room to which he conducted me was evidently the choicest guest-chamber in the house, and it was equally evident that it had not been occupied since the flight of the women. It was in the most exquisite order. No man's hand could have equalled the artistic precision with which the snowy coverings were laid upon the spotless bed. Weary as I was I gazed upon it with a feeling of profound awe. To lie upon that couch which showed the last skilful touch of a vanished woman's hand was a profanation of which, thank Heaven, I was not capable. A luxurious rug which lay on the floor beside the bed better accorded with my feeling of deep humility. I stretched myself upon it, and, completely worn out by the fatigues and mental shocks of the day, swiftly sank into a deep and dreamless sleep.

CHAPTER V.

When I awoke the next morning my mind was clear, and though the recollection of the fact that woman had forsaken man came back to me like the memory of a deeply painful blow, I was still enough like myself to assist Mr. Lister in the task of break-fast-getting with some show of cheerfulness. Break-fast was, however, with the exception of coffee, in the making of which Mr. Lister showed some skill, a repetition of the supper of the previous evening. That it was not again eaten from the original tin cans was, I remember, due to my calling Mr. Lister's attention to the fact that it was said to be dangerous to eat food which had stood for even a brief period of time in open tin cans. This suggestion threw him back unwillingly upon the necessity of dish-washing, for he had to open fresh cans and empty the contents into dishes, which he procured from the pantry. I had observed before during my life that where men, under the stress of circumstances, had assumed the function of dish-washing their dish-cloths speedily took on a grotesque blackness that made them a positively fascinating study. Two or three times after this, in spite of the strange facts which were pressing upon my attention, I found myself absorbed in a kind of rapt, contemplation of Mr. Lister's dish-cloths.

While the meal was in progress I remember that I inquired of Mr. Lister how I could possibly pass the time till the ballots should be cast, for I was conscious of such a horror of home-sickness that I felt I must do something to divert my mind till the terrible suspense should be over. Among other things which I suggested at random, I spoke of visiting some club, as I presumed, without doubt, that there must be several in the town.

" My dear Mr. Carford," said Mr. Lister looking at me sympathetically, " I fear you have only just begun to fathom the depth of the effect of this desolating and singular Strike, if you suppose that men's clubs could possibly exist after woman had forsaken man as she has now done."

"Clubs not exist !" I replied in astonishment. " I should suppose that they would be the only solace in this intolerable gloom."

" I know," said Mr. Lister, " that clubs drew men from their homes before the Strike began, and that they were therefore the source of some domestic trouble from woman's natural jealousy of them. But this you must bear in mind was when the man who went to his club possessed a home made radiant by a patient, beautiful, subjugated woman who awaited his lordly pleasure. Man took the ownership of woman as a matter of course, a desirable and comforting thing to be sure, but still something that was always to be at his beck and ca ll, and therefore a thing for which he was not called upon to make any sacrifice. But when all women, calling each other sisters, withdrew themselves utterly from men with the awful completeness which you now see, there was a fearful reaction. For days men shunned each other as if they were wild beasts, and the thought of assembling together for anything like social interchange, was simply intolerable. The club houses closed immediately."

" But there are the theatres, are there not ? "

" Unfortunately, no," said Mr. Lister. " The theatres made a desperate effort to continue for a time, and even sought to carry on their dramas by having their male actors personate women. But all men fled from this hollow deceit as if it were a ghastly mockery, and the actors were soon stalking before empty seats. The theatres, too, closed."

" But the churches," I said, with a groan ; "surely the churches are accessible ? "

Mr. Lister shook his head. " I am sorry," said he, " to have to deny you that last consolation. When the *Strike* began the churches were suddenly filled to overflowing by men who seldom or never went there before. They seemed to have an unreasoning instinct that the church might afford them some salutary consolation in their unexampled bereavement, but such did not prove to be the case. The truth was, that the ministers themselves felt as much as any class the deep reproach which woman's action cast upon all mankind. They justly felt that teachers though they were, and exemplars though they were supposed to be, they had done even less than far less favoured men to lighten woman's woes. Hence their perfunctory ministrations were without force, utterly inadequate, valueless, and comfortless. It was but a little while before they were feebly talking to empty pews. The churches closed. There are no assemblies of men of any kind except such as are for urging on the completion of the guarantee, and arranging for the casting of the ballots. This, as I told you, will take place the day after to-morrow. Till then I will spend as much time as possible with you, but I must now excuse myself as I have some clerical duties to perform in connection with the coming casting of the ballots."

Having said this, Mr. Lister withdrew from the house, but before doing so he showed me into his well-filled library and promised to return at noon.

Left alone, I essayed to read a volume of new poems, but the face of a woman, not that of any particular woman whom I had known, but a typical face representing all women, hovered persistently, and with reproachful mien, between mine eyes and the page. I cast the book aside. I was strangely nervous. Presently the door-bell rang, and I sprang from my chair in unreasoning terror. For several moments I stood motionless in the centre of the room, muttering only, like Macbeth, "Silence that dreadful bell," but at last arousing myself I went to the door. A boy stood there holding a bundle of papers under his arm, one of which he pertly extended toward me.

" Have a *Bitter Cry*, Mister ? "

" A *Bitter Cry* !" said I petulantly, " what in Heaven's name is that ? "

The boy stared at me for a moment in great surprise, and then said :

"Why it is the paper which the women print every morning; just out, don't yer know?"

"Yes, yes, to be sure," said I, eagerly snatching at the paper which he held toward me. "Give me the *Bitter Cry;* it is the echo of my own soul." The boy stared at me in irreverent wonder, but took the coin I gave him and dashed down the street, while I closed the door and sank into a chair to read. I absorbed rather than read the contents of this strange paper, and this was the first article upon which my eye fell in the *Bitter Cry* ·

"TIMOTHY'S COMING."

Considering the vast number of people who positively did not want little Timothy Totten, but who would have felt infinitely obliged to him if he had utterly stayed away, it is somewhat surprising that he should have ventured into this cold world.

In the first place, his once patient, much-enduring mother, on whose breast he lay alternately squalling and sleeping, cannot be said to have wanted him for she had already borne nine like him, and had long, long ago spent all of her beauty and most of her strength in bearing and caring for Timothy's troublesome predecessors. On her part, then, it must be admitted at the outset, that the bearing of Timothy was simply a common example of the sublime and unsurpassable endurance of woman, combined with the stolid submission of a drudge who sees no escape from her lot. Indeed, the sentiments of Timothy's mother in regard to having children had long ago come to be quite the reverse of those of the Bible Rachel. Instead of saying, " Give me children or I die," the feelings of her heart on this subject, had they found any expression, through many wearisome years, would have taken this form : " Save me from undesired children or I die." Certainly, whoever else in the wide world may have wanted Timothy, it was clear that his mother did not want him.

There is but little less doubt that Timothy's coming was unwelcome to his father, although he observed it with his usual stolid indifference. He was a day- labourer, and already had so many children that he could not support them in anything like comfort or decency ; and for Timothy to come and swell the number of gaping mouths, just when it was so diffi- cult to get work, and labour was so cheap, was decidedly inconsiderate on his part and a downright piece of ill-luck. Then there would be some scanty clothing to be bought for Timothy, and possibly a doctor's bill, and school taxes (provided Timothy had any schooling), and as all these things

loomed up, in prospect, before Timothy's father, he
felt decidedly inhospitable toward Timothy, and as
though, if it were possible, he would like to send him
back where he came from with a surly note of rejection.   Yes, nothing was plainer than that, so far as
Timothy's father was concerned, Timothy was not
wanted.   He was superfluous, or *de trop*, as the French
say.

As Timothy's parents clearly did not want him,
neither can it be said that Timothy's brothers and
sisters wanted him.   They always licked their plates
and fingers very clean at their meagre table, and
sighed ruefully for more, and had they in any way
realized that their already too scanty rations were to
be divided with this new-comer, they would have
clamored louder than anybody against his coming.
Timothy's brothers and sisters, already poorly cared
for, were evidently to gain nothing by his coming,
therefore they could not possibly want him.   He
had better have stayed away so far as they were concerned.

Then there was a silent but general conviction on
the part of the inhabitants of the town in which
Timothy was born, that there were Tottens enough.
Although they might not have held a town-meeting
to take any steps to prevent the coming of Timothy,

if they had had a foreknowledge of it, there is none the less doubt that they regarded his coming as something of a public calamity. They could not expect that Timothy, with his slender chances for education and moral training, would be any improvement on the other nine Tottens, and these had long been looked upon as a grevious infliction. All of the boys had been in the Reform School (the only schooling they ever had) and they were generally accredited with all the hen-roost robbing, water-melon thieving, and miscellaneous trouble-making which took place in the village. The overseer of the poor regarded them as a future inheritance, and even the Census Taker (although a stranger), when he visited the house, looked as though he thought there were too many of them. But perhaps his prejudice may have been owing to the fact that when he got up to wipe his pen Bill Totten moved his chair back a little, and when he sat down again it was not there.

In this swelling tide of remonstrance against the coming of Timothy, it cannot in justice be omitted that even the dogs and cats of his native village, as well as an ancient donkey who grazed upon the Common, would have loudly joined could they have had any intelligent sense of it. Nor would the very frogs in the adjacent marshes, already sorely stoned by Timothy's brothers, have failed to add their dismal, croaking protest to the universal cry. To all these helpless creatures the coming of Timothy simply meant the advent of another tormentor. It was of course utterly impossible that they should want him.

Finally to add to this cloud of objectors to Timothy's coming, a dry and hard-headed and terrible old man by the name of Malthus, had written a book on Population, in which he had proved by many stony facts and immutable figures, that Timothy was not wanted; that, in fact, the world would be greatly better off without him, and that he ought, by every reasonable means, to be discouraged from coming.

All scientific people had great respect for this book, so that if all the conditions had been understood, and a vote had been taken throughout the whole world as to whether Timothy should come or not, there is no doubt that there would have been an overwhelming, universal negative.

But in spite of this general, though silent protest, beginning with his own father and mother, and extending in larger and larger circles to society and the great public, and even including the mute sufferers among the beasts and birds and fishes, Timothy has come, and, as he has thus audaciously braved the public, and defied the very universe, as it were, he must smart for it. Of course he ought to smart for it, and happily his worst enemy could not wish him a greater punishment than that which will befall him. Indeed, we doubt not that if Timothy himself could see the stony path which lies before him, he would bitterly repent of having come, and would cry out as Cain did : " My punishment is greater than I can bear ! "

In the first place, though the milk which he draws from his mother's breast may taste sweet to him, there will be no love in his mother's heart for him, but in its stead a dull sense of hopeless bitterness and abuse, of which, in spite of herself, Timothy will be the scape-goat. Her motherly nature, long deadened to patience and gentleness, will have left only harsh words for Timothy's baby-fretfulness, and rude blows for his baby-mischievousness. Kisses and caresses, a mother's yearning tenderness toward him, a mother's guiding influence over him, a mother's aspirations for him, these Timothy will never know. He will simply be sullenly and peevishly endured, so long as it would be a flagrant crime to expel him, and will be left to his own harmful devices as soon as possible. But then what business had Timothy to come ? He was not wanted.

To his father, little, curious Timothy will simply be as one of the hens or pigs with which he plays around the back door, though of course of nothing like the same importance to the Totten household. Rough words, and blows unalternated by anything kindlier, rags and dirt, cold and hunger, will be his home associations, and his education will be gotten in the street. Brought up to no habits of settled industry, yet impelled to in some way feed fierce passions which have been trained to no other restraint than that of cruel want, what wonder that Timothy becomes the little wild beast which society so much dreaded, and which it was so fearfully interested to have kept back!

But Timothy grows up a predaceous, devouring creature, with life before him which he must get through in some way.

Happily for society, he may be fenced in by jails for a part of the time, and thus gotten rid of, but reappearing again at intervals with accumulated terrors, he pursues his predatory career until, his constitution too broken for active violence, he becomes an unsightly, malodorous, pestiferous tramp, and thus ends his short, eventful history,—a mournful example of retributive justice for coming where he was not wanted.

CHAPTER VI.

" Are you prepared to enjoy the sight of a woman's face ? " was Mr. Lister's first salutation to me as he entered the parlour where I was sitting soon after noon. The copy of *The Bitter Cry* which I was reading fell from my hands. I looked at him search-ingly, thinking that he must be jesting ; but as his face was perfectly serious I concluded that he must refer to the golden time when the "Strike" should be peacefully settled, and woman should happily resume her wonted place in the universe, or a much larger one. I accordingly assured him sincerely that there was no sight on earth that would give me greater pleasure than the sight of a woman, and that I should await the result of the ballot on Monday with feverish impatience.

" But you need not wait the result of the ballot," said Mr. Lister, " for the women have given notice

(43)

that they will pass in procession through the town to-morrow afternoon."

" Do you really mean that the women are going to parade ?" I asked, aghast at this unexpected novelty.

" Well," replied Mr. Lister, " I suppose it might be called a parade, though that term usually carries the idea of a noisy and sensational display, and there will be none of this in the women's passage through the town.   Drums, trumpets, banners, inscriptions, uniforms, speeches, and all the para- phernalia of customary parades will be conspicuously absent.   Clothed in their ordinary garb, the women will exhibit nothing but themselves, in simple, critical sincerity.   Before the ballots are cast they deem it to be both just and proper that man should see, in a simple panorama, exactly the condition of woman as it has been up to to-day.   To-morrow will be Sunday, but as there are no church services the women think it the most proper time for them to walk quietly through the town."

Again it seemed to me that I must be dreaming. Mobs there might have been in history of women clamouring for bread in some oppressed and king- ridden city, but the organization of all the women of Free America into one vast Sisterhood, and their peaceful, speechless procession through streets lined with homes which they had so lately occupied with men, and of which they had been the beacon, was a thought calculated to fill one with speculative awe!

But there were still many things concerning the Strike which I did not understand, and about which I wished to be fully informed before I should witness any such public exhibition. Accordingly, as Mr. Lister was at leisure that afternoon, I gave myself wholly to the task of learning all that I could about this strange situation of the sexes. And first I said :

"It is still exceedingly difficult for me to realize that woman could ever take such a bold step as to practically declare her independence of man. Although I have always known of a few so-called strong-minded women, yet these were not only covertly ridiculed by the men, but by the majority of their own sex as well. It certainly has been generally supposed, and with much apparent reason, that woman, as a whole did not possess that strength and earnestness of character that would ever enable her to carry out any great concerted movement for what she might suppose to be her emancipation. I confess," I continued, with a new and sudden sense of shame, "that now I think of it, I have always regarded woman mysel somewhat as I would a

beautiful toy, the sweetest and most charming acces-
sory to life's happiness, but still so much devoted to
personal ornament as to be forever incapable of any
serious, persistent contention of a principle. The
sight of a gay ribbon or the prospect of a new bonnet
was, it was believed, sufficient to divert woman from
any such vagary as man denominated her 'rights'
to be. Moreover, at the time that I last gave any
attention to the subject, woman's vaulting social
ambition was preternaturally active in seeking and
buying, through marriage, the titled coronets of a
profligate and imbecile nobility. How then could
there be a transformation of character so sudden,
and a precipitate movement requiring such sheer,
desperate earnestness as this Woman's strike?"

"All that you say," replied Mr. Lister, "has been
more or less true of woman's character in the narrow
conditions into which she has been forced in the
past, but you must bear in mind that man as yet has
never seen woman in her deepest and truest
character. The warped and distorted exhibition of woman which has been given up to this
day, has been, in the main, like the acting
of fantastically dressed puppets in a children's
show. It is for the future, dating from this great
Woman's Strike to show the sublime possibilities of

woman's real character. And how in Heaven's name could woman have shown any strength of purpose in the past? Robbed of all other means of employing her brilliant faculties, and bowed down to the doctrine that to look pretty was the chief end of her being, what wonder that her taste for the trappings and frivolities of life should have become abnormally developed? What wonder that being denied all distinction but a vain and showy social distinction, to be obtained only through marriage, she should have aimed at the tinsel stars in that firmament? If you bring up a child on bon-bons and charlotte russe to the exclusion of a more natural diet, you will have a very different kind of being from what you would have if a less artificial regimen were adopted. But after all it was the sudden discovery of her hitherto unsuspected power that transformed, or, rather, gave vent to woman's true character, as quickly as the turning of a wheel. So long as she felt, as she had done for centuries, that she was a beggar, beholden to man's bounty for everything she had, she submitted to being cajoled and wheedled by the airy trifles which he prescribed for her, and which developed only one side of her character. But when woman realized that she was in very truth a queen, that she was man's indispensable complement, and that as such she had an equal right to the free development of all her faculties, and that she possessed the means for enforcing that right, the scales fell from her eyes.   She struck so quickly that it was like the sudden stopping of a clock, but it was the world's pendulum that ceased to move."

" But I cannot conceive," I said, " what woman should want more than you have told me has already been given her.   As I understood you, she already nas every political and economic right that pertains to man.   Does she wish to compel man to do penance for the blackness of his past sins toward her? Does she wish to make man acknowledge that he is inferior to woman? "

" By no means," said Mr. Lister.   " The women were very careful in framing the statement of their grievances, not only to acknowledge but to distinctly proclaim their belief that man was the true head of woman, and as such, was, when a true relationship should be established, entitled to her most loyal recognition.   But while she thus nobly recognised his dynamic character, she none the less declared, as I have told you, that she was his indispensable complement, that she was not a whit less essential than he in the great plan of the universe, and that she was, therefore, clearly entitled to the free development of her own nature, untrammelled by the heavy burdens which have been heaped upon her. Woman, who was made to be the glory of man, claims that man knows nothing whatever of what that glory might be if she existed in an atmosphere of freedom. She would be like the electric light as compared with the tallow candle of our forefathers. It would be a glory that would dazzle mankind."

"But what is this freedom that woman seeks?" I said. "I beg you to tell me at once what this great right is that she calls her MAGNA CHARTA."

"It is," said Mr. Lister, turning and looking me squarely in the face, "the right to the perfect ownership of her own person."

CHAPTER VII.

I did not fully understand the meaning of Mr. Lister's words. "In what respect," I said, "does woman want the ownership of her own person? Does she not have it already?"

"In respect to maternity," he replied.

"I do not understand you," I said; "please explain more fully."

"Well," said Mr. Lister, "the women say that while they are willing, under all proper conditions, to undergo what George Sand grandly called 'the august martyrdom of maternity,' they utterly refuse to have that martyrdom imposed upon them any longer. They say that maternity, multiplied and practically enforced as it is, constitutes the primeval curse that has rested upon them since they were driven out from the Garden of Eden. They say that they can bear that curse no longer, and that the time has come for man, by the same enlightenment that is flooding all other fields of knowledge, to adopt a manner of life that shall remove it."

"In short, they demand, as a final, inalienable right, that man shall give them an irrevocable, per. petual guarantee, that no woman from this time forth and forever, shall be subjected to the woes of maternity without her free and specific consent in all cases."

"What a preposterous idea!" I exclaimed in astonishment. "Upon what ground do they base this extraordinary claim?"

"Simply," replied my friend, "upon the ground that maternity is what George Sand called it, a 'martyrdom.' It puts the life of every woman who enters upon it in real jeopardy. It imperils an exist. ence which is as sweet to woman under true conditions as man's existence is to him. The terrible risks of maternity are woman's and woman's alone. They cannot be shared by man, and woman therefore contends that she alone should freely elect when she should incur those risks. Besides the real peril and physical anguish of maternity, there are the weary months of sleepless watching, of wearing care and wasting anxiety. For man to lightly or indifferently expose woman to such peril and suffering without her free and undoubted assent, is, she claims, worse than the worst form of African slavery, obsolete, barbaric and unchristian."

" Unchristian ! " I feeble echoed, for the sudden opening of such an entirely new field to me for woman's rights confused me so that I mechanically repeated his last word in a kind of stupor, " Unchristian ! "

" Yes, unchristian," he resumed ; " the women quote the saying of St. Paul, 'Love worketh no ill to his neighbour,' and say that man, under the sacred name of love, casts upon woman, who is his nearest and dearest neighbour, the most grievous ills that humanity is capable of bearing. He compels woman to continually run a gauntlet as cruel as the Indian's tomahawk, and multitudes of them sink down before it is run. In the face of such terrible ills as man heaps upon woman, 'the clods of the valley are sweet to her.' See, here is a specimen of the exceeding bitter cry which began to be heard in the public magazines just before the Strike began." And Mr. Lister picked up a magazine which lay on the table, and opening it, pointed to a letter which was contained in an article entitled " To marry or not to marry." This letter was entitled

WHY I CANNOT THANK GOD FOR MY CHILDREN.

Poetically speaking, children are the rose-buds of life ; practically, they are the torments of existence,

I speak from a long and miserable experience. Married at twenty-five, I am now, at thirty-five, the mother of seven children, the eldest nine years, the youngest nine weeks. I am called their mother, but am really their slave. I was once a careless, happy, joyous girl, but my children have made me a fretful, nervous, care-worn woman. All the romance of my life has gone, the poetry of existence has changed to the dullest prose. I live in the midst of quarrelling children, instead of enjoying the society of congenial friends. From Monday morning till Saturday night I am working for my children, yet they show not the slightest gratitude, and make not the least return for all the devotion lavished upon them. Sick or well, am compelled to live in a state of noise and con-fusion, distracting to my nerves and detestable to all my finer feelings.

I do not think my children are exceptionally bad or mischievous; all children are more or less so; and, of course, the more children there are in a family, the more trouble they give. Had the Roman matron, Cornelia, been the mother of seven children, instead of two, she would not have treasured them so highly, and called them her "jewels," as the story says. Instead of being her pets, they would have been the pests of her life, as my seven children are of mine.

I feel—I know I am made for a better, a higher destiny than to be the helpless victim of seven little domestic despots. The delicious bloom of my life is gone for ever. The sweet fancies, the lovely aspirations, the serene happiness that made my girlhood a perpetual joy, will nevermore be mine. My days are passed in a pandemonium from which there is no escape.

I love my husband devotedly, and he deserves all my love, for a kinder, sweeter, tenderer husband never lived ; but, dear as he is to me, had I known that marriage would have made my life what it is, I never would have married him.

A Miserable Mother.

" But surely," said I, after I had finished reading the letter, "this must be a very extreme case. There are women who prefer large families, and who think the rearing of them no hardship."

" I scarcely think that it can be said that they do not consider it any hardship to rear such families," replied Mr. Lister. "I remember hearing my grandmother say once that for nineteen years she did not know a single night's unbroken rest. She had nine children. But if there be now and then a woman who is content to become a mere propagative drudge, the great majority of them are not. They have tastes and aspirations of their own, and do not care to merge them all in children. But I beg you to remember that the essential point which woman seeks to gain in her controversy with man on this subject, is the acknowledgment of her undeniable right to the complete ownership of her own person, whether the children she bears may be many or few. And on this point I assure you that woman is in dead earnest. She will have this ownership of her own person or she will allow the race to lapse from the face of the earth. Malthus certainly never foresaw any such fearful contingency. It can be compared to nothing in the entire history of the human race, unless it be the stopping of the sun at Joshua's command."

"But if woman is granted this astonishing right," I said, "will she not seek to escape the burden of maternity to such a degree as to seriously diminish the population?"

"Of that," replied Mr. Lister, "we have no certain means of judging. Nor does it, indeed, concern the principle of justice involved. *Fiat justitia ruat cælum.* But if woman is really given her freedom, her innate instincts will undoubtedly expand naturally and strongly, and certainly the desire for children is strongly implanted in her.

But her children from this time forward, if she ever has any, will be only children which are desired, and to the bearing of which she has joyfully consented. This simple condition alone must mark the beginning of a new race."

As at many times before during the last two days, I could scarcely persuade myself that I was not dreaming. The discovery of this astounding separation between the sexes, the strange intelligence that woman, by a simple edict of her own, had solved the social evil and swept it summarily into the limbo of the abominations of the past, and now this undreamed of right to say whether she should bear children or not !

I knew not what to say; the world seemed turned to sudden and inexplicable chaos; a thousand difficulties and perplexities presented themselves to my mind, and I was about to excuse myself and go out into the street to cool my heated brain, when a dull, heavy alarm bell sounded in the town.

"It is fire," said Mr. Lister, springing from his chair. "Good God! what if it should be among the buildings occupied by the women!"

Even as he spoke there came the sound of the swelling, hurrying rush and tread that springs up in the track of a dread ravager. We rushed tumultu-ously into the street,

CHAPTER VIII.

I had known the terror that seizes upon the heart at the sudden alarm of devastating fires before. I had been awakened by such alarms from a peaceful sleep at midnight. I had felt rather than heard the dull vibration of heavy axes beating in barred doors to break an entrance into buildings where fierce fires were raging. Through the rents made by frenzied blows, I had caught intermittent gleams of licking tongues of fire curling upward with devouring eagerness. I had heard the blood-curdling cries of the watchmen. I had witnessed the mad galloping of the engines. I had seen the dismay of the terrified occupants of burning buildings suddenly shaken from sound slumber, and rushing almost naked into the streets. None of these things were strange to me, and still I trust I may never know again the sickening, contagious terror I felt when I reached the street and knew that the fire was located in the buildings which the women had chosen for their retreat.

No one told me this.   I instinctively felt it the moment I joined the throng of hatless, coatless, pale-faced men who were hurrying with frantic, but speechless haste toward the bridge which led to the women's home.   All the treasures of the earth were but as dust compared with those that were in jeopardy on that hill-side.

A groan of relief escaped the lips of those about me as we drew near the noble group of buildings, which the women had chosen for their home, and saw that the one that was on fire stood at such a distance from the others that it did not greatly en-danger them.   The building which was on fire was in fact built for a hospital, and was, therefore, pur-posely kept aloof from the rest.   But though the anxiety lest there should be a general conflagration among the women's quarters was assuaged, the progress of the flames in the burning buildings was sufficiently terrifying.   Flames had begun to dart intermittently from an upper window, and a huge column of black smoke was heavily drifting into the starlit sky.

It is true that women, as a rule, are not cool and clear-headed in the presence of the peril of sudden fire, though it is also true that many men are not more so. This fact it appeared had been clearly recognized by the women, and only the trained women nurses, who were employed in the hospital, —those noiseless, efficient, self-possessed, self-deny- ing creatures, who pass their gentle lives in the dim twilight of sick-rooms,—had been allowed by the women to remain near the building after the fire had been discovered. With quiet celerity these trained nurses had got the greater part of the patients safely out of the building before a man arrived. All was calm- ness, action, and self-restraining nerve. It was only when in response to the dire summons of the alarm bell, the impetuous wave of men surged up the hill and around the building, that there was anything like mad disorder, and fruitless panic. Not a man stopped for a instant after reaching the burning building, but plunged madly into its interior. The halls became choked with them, they stumbled over each other on the staircases, with demoniac strength they forced all oppposing doors from their hinges, wildly groping through the blinding smoke after any woman that might possibly have been left. Every instant brought fresh panting relays of men, who disappeared into the building as swiftly as those who had gone before them. Suddenly, in the midst of the dire and increasing confusion, a tall and slender woman emerged from the smoke at the broad entrance. Great masses of chestnut hair were held back from her pure, impassioned face by some chance fastening caught up at the moment. There was a lofty serious-ness and a noble self-possession in her stately hear-ing that made the desperate men who were pressing toward the entrance pause and draw back as if suddenly confronted by an angelic apparition. She had raised her hands to press them against the breasts of the men who were tumultuosly advancing, but there was no need. A sudden hush and calm had fallen on them all at sight of her. But the words that she spoke sounded as strangely as the words of an incongruous dream

" Where are the engines ? " she said quietly.

Where indeed ? Up to this time there had been a constant arrival of men who were more like madmen than anything else, but there had not appeared the slightest sign of any appliances, either for putting out the fire or for rescuing those in peril. The strong panting men whom this beautiful young woman addressed in such quiet but earnest tones, hung their heads upon their breasts speechless and abashed. The truth was apparent. At the first sound of the alarm of fire in the woman's quarters every man in the town, filled with a sickening fear, and torn with a mad anxiety lest woman should really be lost forever past all recovery, had rushed headlong to the spot, leaving prudence, caution and forethought utterly behind him. The one mad idea which con-trolled them all was to rush into the flames and tear their beloved away from them with their own powerful hands. They had left the means of staying the fire behind them. The woman saw it all in an instant, and in a voice which was both quiet and imperious, she said:

"Go back at once and get the engines, and be qu'ck."

The men did not need a second word. Seizing horses which were at hand they disappeared across the bridge in sufficient numbers to bring all the ap-pliances for rescue and for putting out fire that were in the town.

But in the meantime the flames had not stayed. They had broken out in a lower storey, and all the men who had reached the top storey in their frantic search for any woman who might be there, were imprisoned by the fire which enveloped the stair-cases. To add to the terror of the situation, it was discovered that a lame girl who had been a patient in the ward on the top floor of the building, had not been seen and could not be found. She must be in the building. This discovery was a signal for a fresh rush of heroic, reckless men into the flames in search for her at any peril. But the same magnificent woman who had sent for the engines stopped them with a command that they could not disobey.

" You will only throw your lives away," she said; " the men who are already in the building will take care of the lame girl if it is possible to save either."

As she said this a great sympathetic cry arose from the crowd who were gazing anxiously up at the burning building.

The men who were imprisoned by the fire, about twenty in number, had gained the roof and were triumphantly holding up in their strong arms the lame girl. The flames had driven them to one end of the building and appeared to be surrounding them, leaving only one corner unexposed.

Merciful Heavens, would the engines and scaling ladders never arrive!

Steadily the flames advanced, but fortunately the night was perfectly still, so that their progress was slow. The men on the roof, falling back foot by foot, had at last placed the lame girl at the least exposed spot and formed a hollow square around her presenting only their own dauntless breasts to the destroyer that threatened her.

"Call to them," said the woman who had directed the men, "tell them to have courage, courage!" The strong man to whom she spoke essayed to do as she told him. He hoarsely cried out, but his voice weakened and broke into weeping. He was completely unnerved.

At this terrible moment there came a noise like rolling thunder on the bridge, and in another instant all the appliances for quenching fire and for rescue were in the eager hands of a hundred feverish workers. Deluging streams of water poured on to the flames which surrounded the band on the roof. Ladders were quickly hoisted, and borne in strong arms, arms to whom woman was precious as never before, the lame girl, without the smell of fire upon her garments, was gently placed upon the ground beside the woman. As they embraced each other I heard the lame girl call her " Allegra." The men who had been her companions, and who had been tenderly assisted to the ground, eyed them at a little distance with haggard, pathetic interest.

It was three o'clock in the morning when Mr. Lister and I, in company with a host of wan and forlorn-looking men, re-crossed the bridge and betook ourselves toward our homes. With faces blackened by smoke, their clothing torn and burnt, their beards singed, and without coats, hats or shoes, they looked like the stern and ravaged remnant of some historic Old Guard returning from a desperate assault. Jaded as I was, I remember that the thought of burning Moscow and the desperate, heroic retreat of Marshall Ney and his valiant rear guard, passed vaguely through my mind. But at the homes toward which these men were turning, there were no women to meet them with tears of love and pity, and to bind up their wounds with tender hands! They sternly entered their empty homes in silence. But so utterly exhausted was I with the excitement of the night, that this strange, pathetic spectacle did not greatly move me. Mr. Lister and I, without exchanging a word, staggered up the steps of his house like drunken men.

But though I was nearly worn out with fatigue, the thought of going to my room and of being alone with my thoughts was utterly intolerable. I knew that I could not sleep. The excitement of the struggle with fire in which we had just been engaged the anticipation of the curious parade which I was to witness on the morrow, to say nothing of the strange revelations which had crowded upon me in the past two days, made sleep a sheer impossibility. And yet it seemed to me that I must have some diversion or I should go mad. What to do I knew not.

As I could think of no other diversion, I deter. mined, as a last resort, to go to my room and spend the night in reading. To do so I had to go by Mr. Lister's room, the door of which, for the first time when I had passed it, stood wide open. As I chanced to raise my eyes to the wall opposite the door, I stopped in sudden awe, as if confronted by the shrine of a Madonna. An exquisite oil portrait of a woman hung there, and I saw at a glance that it was the beautiful, imperious creature who had such a magic influence in controlling the men at the fire.

There were the same large eyes looking upward from under a drift of gold-flecked chesnut hair. Her expression was that of eager, almost prophetic antici-pation. A ravishing smile of hope and confidence was on her slightly parted lips, and the velvet curve of a resolute but womanly chin showed deep courage and devotion. This, then, was undoubtedly Mr. Lister's prospective bride. If I could but hear the love story of this man and woman what a diversion it would be !

I determined to fearlessly ask Mr. Lister to tell me his love story that night.

CHAPTER IX.

My absorption had been so deep in gazing at the beautiful portrait that I had not observed that Mr. Lister had come up the stairs and was standing silently behind me.

"Is she not beautiful?" he whispered. "Was she not magnificent at the fire?"

"She was magnificent, she is beautiful," I replied, deliberately turning and facing him. He was a man fair to look upon, and one that could not fail to be pleasing to a woman's eye. He was slightly above the medium height. His well-knit and athletic frame was surmounted by a well-shaped, intellectual head, which was crowned with clustering brown hair. A strong, well-shaped nose, rather deep-set, intro-spective eyes, and a refined and sensitive mouth, made a countenance of more than usual interest. Just now it appeared somewhat wan and heavy from watching, but his was evidently one of those gifted natures that are subject to sudden, brilliant kindling, like the cheery flame which sometimes leaps from a smouldering fire.

" Surely," I thought, "this woman could not but have deeply loved this man. And yet she left him for the sake of woman." As this thought passed through my mind, I unconsciously looked from my friend to the portrait, and back to him again.

" What are you thinking of?" said Mr. Lister. "That portrait is Allegra Alliston. You saw her at the fire to-night. She was to have been married to me on Monday, if it had not been for the Woman's Strike."

"I am thinking," I said slowly, replying to his question, "that I cannot sleep, and that I would like above all things at this moment to hear the love story of Justin Lister and Allegra Alliston."

Mr. Lister, without seeming to hear what I said, took me by the arm and drew me into his room. He pressed me into an easy chair, and sinking down into a cosy window-seat opposite, he said, as if continuing what he had said before:

" Yes, we were to have been married on Monday, the very day when the ballots are to be cast that will decide the fate of the human race. But when the Strike came, she said she could not allow her per-

sonal pleasure to stand between her and the obtain-
ing for woman of rights that were so plainly hers.
She is a noble enthusiast in the cause of woman, and
though she was in the midst of preparing her bridal
outfit when the Strike was proposed, she brushed it
aside as if it were cobwebs. She said that she felt
that the supreme hour of woman's destiny had come,
and to miss it were to be a renegade from everything
noble.

" She is beautiful," continued Mr. Lister, glancing
fondly toward the portrait, " but her irresistible
charm is in what she says and in her manner of
saying it. Although she is simple and pure as a lily,
she is continually saying unexpected things, things
that give you a start of surprise, upset your conven-
tionalism and put you into a stimulating glow in
spite of yourself.

" It was a genuine case of love at first sight, or
rather of love at the first meeting, for it was really so
dark when I first met her that I could not distinguish
her features clearly. She does not belong to the
wealthy class, and she gave music lessons in order to
support herself and her two little brothers. She
called here at this house at twilight one evening with
an acquaintance of my mother to see if she could obtain
a pupil in my sister. It was dusk when I casually

entered the parlour where they sat. The lamps had not been lighted. I was feeling rather dull and listless from the fatigues of the day, and scarcely noticed Miss Alliston after the formal introduction. I sat down rather indifferently, preoccupied with my own thoughts, while she continued conversation with my mother. Suddenly I remember hearing her say in answer to some inquiry of my mother, that she was a 'Yankee through and through.' It was a simple thing to say, but, good Heavens! what subtle power there was in her! That speech aroused me as if I had been suddenly shaken from sleep! Two or three minutes later she said something in her bright, bracing, dashing way, that made me feel as one feels who has had a mirth-provoking tumble. Before I had been in her society ten minutes, I was talking to her, and was like a man who was recklessly swallowing wine, glass after glass! When, at last, I followed her to the carriage in which her friend had brought her, I loved her as madly as a man ever loved a woman. I could have kissed her from head to foot. The touch of my hand on her waist as I helped her into the carriage that evening! —it thrills me now. I can never forget that, if the Strike should be continued and I should never see her again.

" After that evening I can truly say that I never went out of my way to seek her. I know not what the instinct was that restrained me. It is one of those things about the human heart that is past finding out. It is true that I thought of her every day, and oftentimes I cast a wistful glance toward the street in which I knew she lived, but as I had nothing but my love for me to call there, I could not go.

" And that period when I loved her unknown to herself or to any human being is treasured up in my soul as one of the purest and sweetest in existence. I really discovered, past any doubt, that there is a depth of exquisite joy in simply loving, whether the person you love knows of your love or not, or whether she return it or not,   It was like the secret discovery of a clear bubbling spring beside which my world-wearied spirit could linger in purest contentment and serenest joy.   Love can distil its exquisite perfume in your own soul, whether it is wafted to others or not.   It was when I was feeding upon the sweet bliss of this discovery that this verse formed itself almost unconsciously in my mind:

"Hast thou found Love in all the sphere?
    Then know it by this perfect token,
    Thy love was never known or spoken,
    And still thy joy was all unbroken :
Such love the stars revere !

" Sometimes I fancied that she could hear my soul calling to her in the voiceless night, and that her soul made sweet responses.

" But though I refrained almost conscientiously from seeking Allegra Alliston, fate seem to continually throw us together without the slightest design on our part. Do you want to know the surest sign of love in the world ? It is when you can tell every time at which you have seen her whom you love, without missing a single instance. It may have been nothing more than a passing glimpse of her face in a prosaic street car but it is as firmly photographed in your memory as if you had held her tightly in your arms. I could not only remember every glimpse I had ever had of Allegra Alliston during the next six months, but I could repeat, with the accuracy of a phono-graph, every word she had said in my hearing.

"Once during this time I was passing a house in which she gave music lessons, although I did not know it until I heard her rapturous voice singing. I had never heard the song before, but being sung by her it was indelibly fixed in my memory. See, I can repeat it now :

"COME BACK.

" 'Come back I ' from many a broken home
There comes a voice of sad endeavour

To bring the loved ones back who roam
To bring them back to dwell forever.
"'Come back, dear ones, Love calls you home,
No more to doubt, no more to roam
Come back—come back.

"'Tis bourne across the ocean's main
And blown along the desert's tract
In words which tell earth's deepest pain.
Come back! ye loved ones, O come back.
"Come back, dear ones, Love calls you home,
From her warm arms no more to roam,
Come back—come back.

"'Dear ones come back to that sweet home
Where loves strong ties are parted never,
No more to weep, no more to roam,
Come back and dwell in peace forever
"'Come back dear ones, Love calls you home,
From her fond breast no more to roam,
Come back—come back.'"

"As I said, although Miss Alliston did not enter our house again for a long time after that first evening, fate threw us together in the most unexpected ways. At last when I had not seen her for some weeks, I started to drive to a village a few miles distant on a business errand. As I drove along the lonely country road, I was in an exceedingly happy frame of mind. The solitude and a radiant fragrant autumn day were favourable to my deep enjoyment of the incense that burned upon the secret altar of my soul. I remember feeling a special glow of satisfaction that morning that I was content simply to have Love as a noble guest in the chambers of my heart. I asked no other gifts from her hands.

"As I made a turn in the road, which was lined with woods on one side, I noticed to my surprise a woman dressed in black picking her way somewhat daintily along the muddy roadside at some distance ahead of me. By the way, don't you like to see women dressed in black? It is my favourite dress. There is a rich grace and dignity about women dressed in black that seems wanting in any other colour. Their throats are so white, and their forms so sweetly and seriously graceful; it makes them doubly mysterious and captivating to me.

"Of course when I saw this lady walking by the roadside, I decided at once to offer her a seat in my carriage. But I had not the slightest idea who she might be, nor indeed did I spend a moment's thought upon it. Judge then of my electrifying surprise when I had stopped the carriage, and she had for the first time turned her face toward me, to see that it was Allegra Alliston! I felt as if I were in a dream as I helped her into the carriage, and she was apparently as much surprised as I was. But the explanation of her being there was very simple.

She had obtained a new pupil in the sleepy village toward which we were going, and as she had no other means of getting there, she was heroically walking, although the distance was five miles. .

"Do you believe in the sharpness of woman's intuition? If there is such a thing, I told Allegra Alliston that I loved her a thousand times during that short ride. Not in words, or by any intent, but—I made a desperate effort to appear natural and unconcerned. There was a rich glow upon her face from walking. I drew the carriage robes around her and asked her if she was dressed warmly enough to ride. I tried to hide my secret, but every motion I made, every word I uttered seemed to give it hopelessly away. I became positively frightened, for it seemed as if at every turn of the carriage wheels I was saying, 'I love you, I love you, I love you!'

"As we drew near the little village, Miss Alliston said something about its dulness, and I replied that possibly it might become a populous city some day; that sometimes such places, after long lying in lethargy, were found to possess unsuspected advantages, and sprang into sudden life and importance.

"'But it will be after our time,' she said, 'some

hundreds of years from now. Where shall we be then ? ' "

" I did not premeditate at all what I said in reply to this. A man who is deeply in love has a tongue that is set on a hair trigger. I talked without knowing what I was saying.

" ' If we meet in another sphere, Miss Alliston, and I confess I indulge myself in the perhaps foolish hope that congenial souls will meet and recognize each other hereafter, I shall have something to tell you about this strange and far-distant earth-life. I assume that there will be no such artificial trammels there as to prevent me from speaking to you without fear.'

" ' Oh,' said she, with the charming audacity that s so characteristic of her, ' tell me now. A woman, you know, can neither keep a secret, nor rest till she finds one out.'

" ' Tell you !' I cried, with a sudden burst of vehemence that was almost like anger. ' I have told you a thousand times. Oh, God ! I have tried to hide it, and yet you know as well as if I had shouted it to the hills, that I love you unutterably, that I have never ceased loving you since I first saw you.'

" The reins had fallen from my hands and the

horse had stopped in uncertainty. She caught the reins, but strange as it may seem, this burst of vehemence produced something very much like it in her. Her great eyes turned upon me with a blazing light which I had never seen in them before.

"'And you, too!' she cried, 'do you blame me for my skill at concealing my heart? Since when has woman been permitted to manifest her feelings toward man in the slightest degree? You could not hide your love because man has always had the liberty to express it. But woman, compelled for ages to stifle every heart-beat, has learned her unnatural lesson too well. Like the stoical Indian she can bear her torture without flinching. But,— but,' and her splendid voice began to falter, 'I have loved you none the less.' And we were both crying.

"Had a traveller been concealed on that country road he would have been puzzled to see a young man and woman sitting in a carriage, and apparently quarrelling at one moment, but at the next locked in each other's arms and smothering each other with kisses."

CHAPTER X.

Mr. Lister paused a moment in the narration of a story to which I had listened with absorbing interest, and then said:

"Ah me, that was eight years ago."

"Eight years ago?" I exclaimed, "what a long courtship!"

"It did not seem long to us. We had both discovered from much observation of our married friends that courtship was the true elysium in every one's life, and a far happier state than marriage. Noting this we asked each other why we should not prolong this happy season. In it we realised that each was to the other a delightful and never-ending mystery. We saw that in courtship we had a feeling of deep reverence for each other which was almost wholly wanting among married people. In courtship we each felt that love was generous condescension in the other. I did not feel that I was at all worthy of

(77)

her, and she did not feel that she was worthy of me. We were inexpressibly sacred objects in each other's eyes, and above all things we desired to remain so.

"Besides, to tell the truth, we saw some terribly dark spots in marriage from which we shrank as from the contemplation of the slimy things in a pool. It seemed 'filled with the habitations of cruelty!' She confided to me that she had a schoolmate, a dear friend, who had been married a few years before. She was a radiant, fragrant being, fitted by every gift of Nature to shed light and perfume, joy and laughter wherever she went. But alas, she was not physically adapted to the fearful treadmill of enforced maternity. After twice becoming a mother and barely escaping the ordeal with her life, she was warned that another risk of that kind would undoubtedly have a fatal termination. And this innocent, helpless being, with a sword hanging over her bright young life, went on her way scattering gentle words and loving deeds along her blackly shadowed path. But O, the pity of it! the sword fell. Within a year she was a martyr to the fearful Moloch which yawns continually over woman's life. She escaped by death from a life so fraught with cruel suffering, so filled with unutterable indignities, that the wonder is that woman did not strike long ago!

" In the ecstasy of our love Allegra Alliston and I vowed that we would never take part in a system that permitted such unspeakable cruelty. We chose rather to enjoy the quiet pleasures of courtship and be satisfied with them."

" And yet," said I, "you had decided to get married. You said that Miss Alliston was preparing her wedding-dress at the time of the commencement of the Strike."

" Oh," said Mr. Lister, "the great discovery of Zugassent opened up a manner of life by which married people could preserve their sacred reverence for each other, and make the state of courtship a perpetual one. When we saw that we could enter into the joys of marriage without ravaging each other like wild beasts, we had no longer any reason for not doing so. We decided to get married at once."

" But," said I, as soon as I could speak, "you talk as though I knew all about Zugassent and his discovery, when in fact I never heard of either."

" Why," said Mr. Lister, " it was the wonderful discovery of Zugassent that emboldened the women to strike, and gave a logical basis for their movement.

Before that discovery was made, much as they desired the Magna Charta which they are now asking, they were reasonable, and scarcely saw how man could give it. The problem seemed too deep and intricate for any possible solution. But when Zugassent's discovery was made, they saw that it took away from man all excuse for withholding this right. They demanded it at once."

At this fresh promise of an utterly unlooked-for revelation, I felt a despairing kind of anger. Could this be the same world in which I had for thirty-five years lived a sober and commonplace life? Mr. Lister had already, in the few days which I had spent with him, dazed me and amazed me with the stunning character of the intelligence which he had conveyed to me. Did he wish to craze me also? Unconsciously I put my hand to my head and stared at him in helpless, pathetic reproach. But he did not appear to be conscious of my feelings. At last when I had mastered myself enough to speak calmly, I said:

"I wish that you would tell me all about Zugassent and his discovery. I have been trying to find out the causes of this singular Strike, and now I hear for the first time that it was assisted by a great discovery about which I am entirely ignorant. I entreat you to tell me who Zugassent was and what was his discovery?"

"Zugassent," said Mr. Lister, and his lip quivered, and a sudden moisture sprang into his eyes as he spoke, "was a pure and noble soul who believed that everything that was of human interest was worthy of conscientious, painstaking study, and that everything which involved human happiness or misery was a legitimate field for honest effort for improvement. The appalling sum of misery resulting to woman from the present system of marriage, and indirectly to men and children as well through the too great division of the means of subsistence, filled his heart with a divine compassion. It is said that his attention was first called to this subject by observing the suffering of his own wife. That he should be the cause of producing such unavailing suffering became a source of deep disquietude to him. He resolved rather than to pursue a course so fraught with evil to woman, to return to the simple relations of courtship. He fondly loved his wife, but he had firmly decided to content himself with the purely Platonic and spiritual pleasures of her society. Being, however, a natural thinker and a man of studious tastes and habits, he could not help revolving the problem in his thoughts, much wondering at its mind-baffling character. The more he pondered the matter the more was he struck with the astounding anomaly presented by this scientific age. He saw that the explorer, the discoverer and the pioneer were pushing their caravans and wagon-trains into every unmapped land on the globe, and steering their barks into every unknown sea. Applauded by the world, they were daring the burning fevers of Central Africa, and leaving their bones for other as determined discoverers to find in the frozen regions of the North Pole. He saw that in the domain of Science, and Art, and Invention an innumerable host of patient, earnest workers and thinkers, lured on by the highest rewards which Earth could offer, were burning midnight oil in an agonizing search after improvement. Consuming brain and nerve with unremitting and profligate energy, these toilers after newer and better ways were fast robbing the earth of all its material secrets. Even in Religion the rock-bound creeds of hoary churches were being diligently revised and unscrupulously altered to adapt them to the new light of a refulgent present. Everywhere there was light, change, improvement, discarding the old and adopting the newer and better, except in the social relation of man and woman. This alone remained, not, indeed, unquestioned, but unexplored and unimproved, the one stationary fixture of an obsolete and decrepit past. Zugassent saw with absolute and increasing wonder that none of the new light which was flooding the world was allowed to penetrate this dark Continent. A superstition as black, as unreasoning, as utterly inconsistent as that which compelled Galileo to retract his affirmation about the earth's motion, shrouded this dark Continent and forbade any student to set foot therein. No matter how pure the motive, no matter what misery it was sought to alleviate, the leperous cry, ' Unclean! Unclean!' was ready to be raised at any one who should seek to direct some of the unstinted light of a marvellous age into this dark domain of ignorance and injustice. To be sure, every one freely acknowledged that black and mephitic vapours were continually arising from this great uncleared land. Every one marvelled that it could be so enveloped in darkness, when there was life and light, change and improvement continually going on about it. The wailing which came from this dark Continent was a source of continual commiseration on the part of every one, and the recitals of the heartrending cruelties, the pestilential scandals, and the shameful deeds that were enacted in this dark country, and which far exceeded those of Siberia, constituted a large and staple part of the intelligence of the newspapers. An age which boasted that it could foretell its weather, and measure the stars, and girdle the earth, was supinely and superstitiously content to let the relation between man and woman remain an unstudied and unimproved part and parcel of a benighted and slave-driving past! As if beyond anything else that concerned mankind, his relations to woman, next to his relation to his Creator, were not the most important, the most deserving of free scientific and conscientious research, and the one supreme improvement for which the world's highest premiums should be offered."

There was a choking sound in Mr. Lister's throat. He seemed like one about to weep. But he continued,

"Zugassent saw all this. He fully realized that the man who conscientiously gave his mind to the study of these problems, who honestly sought to illumine this great department of human life with some of the light which was being prodigally shed elsewhere, would be reviled and misunderstood. He knew that the impure would call him impure, and that the thoughtless would jeer at him. He knew that many good people, still somewhat bound

by the fast-failing chains of superstition, would sus-
pect his motives, and would deem any investigation
of this subject unlawful. Nevertheless, Zugassent
determined that in no other field of human interest
was discovery and improvement so wofully and piti-
fully lacking, and that though for the present, his
name might be covered with obloquy, future genera-
tions would respect his effort if this did not. He
therefore resolved, with all the desperate earnestness
of a man who is preparing to take leave of his home
and friends'forever, to light his humble torch and go
alone into the murky caverns of this dark Continent.
He would, if possible, open some part of it to the
light of day. He did so, and his beneficent discovery, but just beginning to be made known, has
placed him at the very head of those who have
honestly and successfully toiled for the betterment
of the human race."

"And Zugassent's discovery?" said I, eagerly.
But the rays of the morning sun were bursting in at
the window. It was broad daylight.

Mr. Lister arose. His face was wet with tears.
"My dear Mr. Carford," said he, "have you forgotten that to-day is Sunday, and that we are to
witness the woman's parade this afternoon? It is
absolutely necessary that we should take some rest

before that. I will give you Zugassent's book and let him speak for himself."

I went to my room and lay down upon the rug. As I passed along the hall I heard Mr. Lister singing the snatches of a song as he prepared himself to rest; and as I drifted into sleep, it was with the words of his song running in my mind :

> Love lingers not where sorrow dwells,
>   She cannot bide the downcast face ;
> Where laughter rings like golden bells
>   Is Love's abiding place.

> Love follows those, though seeming vain,
>   Who gild life's path with faith and hope ;
> She smiles on those who smile again,
>   Not on the misanthrope.

>   Love smiles on those who smile again,
>   Not on the misanthrope.

CHAPTER XI.

It was noon when I awoke from the deep stupor rather than sleep into which I had plunged. How swiftly, when one is waked out of sleep, comes back the engrossing joy or grief which lay upon his heart when sleep stole it away! But at this awakening I was conscious only of a strange, dull sense of grief. I was for some time too much dazed to analyze my sensations or to fully realize what had occured in the past few days, and on attempting to rise I found that I was stiff and sore, as after unusual exertion.

The copy of the *Bitter Cry* which I had left in my room the day before lay on the floor. It served to recall to me the reality of the strange circumstances into which I had fallen. I remember that a humorous account of the Button Manufacturers' plea before the Woman's Executive Committee to allow mankind to continue the use of buttons, first caught my attention, and that afterward I read the following:

"LOVE WORKETH NO ILL TO HIS NEIGHBOUR."

It was with more than his usual unction that the Rev. Jonathan Holworthy announced his text one bright Sunday May morning, to the distinctly rural congregation of Middle-brook.

Smoothing out with one soft, plump hand the pages of the large Bible which lay on the pulpit cushion in front of him, he raised the other impressively, and shot a comprehensive and penetrating glance toward his humble and unpretending auditors. This glance, proceeding from under a pair of shaggy eyebrows, and passing over the gold-rimmed spectacles set low on his nose, was intended as a kind of preliminary shot to awaken in the congregation any who were sleepily disposed, and to draw the attention of each one of his parishioners to the unusually "great effort" which he was about to make. And it must be confessed that this impressive manner and sharp glance had the effect of uncomfortably arousing several rather torpid individuals who had settled themselves comfortably into their pews, and on whom the ministrations of the Rev. Mr. Holworthy had usually the effect of the droning of a bumble bee in August.

"Wonder if we're going to have another 'Great Awakenin'' such as I remember forty years ago,' said Deacon Weatherby to himself. "The minister 'pears to have something powerful on his mind.'

And Deacon Weatherby, like several others in the congregation, shook off the sleepy fit which usually came on with great regularity as soon as he had settled himself in his pew. He now sat bolt upright, with an air of alertness that he did not manifest even in the numerous keen horse trades in which he participated, and in which he was always credited with coming off " first best."

The Rev. Jonathan Holworthy, who had stood in silence with his hand on the page of the open Bible, critically surveying the assembled farmers and village folks of Middlebrook, appeared to be well satisfied with the effect of his unusual impressiveness. He therefore proceeded to deliberately announce his text, repeating it twice, slowly, as if each word were heavy, and he had to lift it with an effort: " Love-worketh-no-ill-to-his-neighbour — Love-worketh-no-ill-to-his-neighbour."

Having thus delivered his text with much solemnity, and having apparently divided it in his mind under several heads, the Rev. Mr. Holworthy first addressed himself to the subject of Love. But Love cannot be said to have been the particular game which he was hunting in the great oratorical effort which he had planned for himself that morning. Beyond a few general platitudes interspersed with Scriptural quotations, he did not, therefore, expatiate upon this branch of his discourse. It was only when he came to consider the subject of " his neighbour " that he may be said to have really struck the trail, and to have warmed up in the pursuit of his argument. "Who is my neighbour ? " he suddenly demanded, with so much imperative force, that a half-witted young man, who sat in the front row, promptly replied, " Ike Hunniwell, the infidel."

This reply to the minister's inquiry produced a half-frightened smile on the faces of some of the congregation. It must, however, be admitted, that in general to the simple-minded farmers of Middlebrook, unaccustomed as they were to much allegory or metaphor, their "neighbours" were simply the plain, hard-featured, but kindly, men and women who lived on the farms adjoining their own, and the but little more stylish men and women whose humble homes lined the streets of Middlebrook.

But the Rev. Mr. Holworthy was looking for a

very different neighbour from any of these, and he therefore only frowned at the reply of half-witted Ira Aliter.

And in pursuit of this anomalous, hypothetical neighbour, the Rev. Mr. Holworthy may then be said to have proceeded to compass sea and land. He sought him in the far-off jungles of India, on the trackless wastes of Africa, among the nomadic hordes of Tartary, and in the rigorous confines of Siberia. No land known to be inhabited by the human race was too distant or too inaccessible for the broad sweep of his resistless benevolence to reach. Indeed, if man had been amphibious, there is but little doubt that he would have dragged the sea in the ardour of his all-pervading search for this neighbour to whom "love" was to "work no ill." But as man did not occupy the depths of the sea, the Rev. Mr. Holworthy contented himself with traversing, in his astonishing mental flight, all the most distant and uncivilized countries known to the geographer

And in all these far-away places, some of which the bewildered farmers of Middlebrook had never heard of before, the Rev. Mr. Holworthy had no difficulty in triumphantly finding "his neighbour"; and having thus found "his neighbour" at the uttermost ends of the earth, the Rev. Mr. Holworthy un-

ceremoniously haled him as it were, taking him by
the nape of the neck, metaphorically speaking, and
holding him up for the dumbfounded farmers of
Middlebrook to gaze upon.

Having thus shown to the undiscriminating inhabitants of Middlebrook who their real " neighbours" were, the Rev. Mr. Holworthy proceeded
to invest these " neighbours" with the garments
made by the local branch of the Missionary
Society, putting these garments on to these imag-
inary " neighbours" somewhat as a constable
would clap handcuffs on to a miserable wretch who
had long eluded justice.   Thus, the Rev. Mr. Holworthy, to his own satisfaction, showed to his congregation that through the efforts of their local
branch of the Missionary Society they were working
no ill but positive good to their "neighbours" in the
antipodes.   He then indulged in much self-gratula-
tory and flowery complacence, assuring his congregation that they were sublimely proving the Apostle
Paul's great sentence that " Love worketh no ill to
his neighbour."

In the minister's pew, a little way to the left of the
front of the pulpit, sat a pale and faded ghost of a
woman.   She sat in the middle of the pew, and on
her right, looking very uneasy in tight jackets and

broad white collars, sat five stout boys. On her left, in stiffly starched sun-bonnets and white aprons, were four prim and meek-faced girls. Mrs. Holworthy was looking more than commonly pale and fragile on this particular May morning. The delicate blue veins in her white throat and in her slender wrists showed plainly. Two or three times that morning Mr. Holworthy had sent peremptory word out from his study that the children must be kept more quiet, as he was putting the finishing touches on his great sermon, " Love worketh no ill to his neighbour." Two or three times that morning, while undergoing the fatigues of preparing the children for church, Mrs. Holworthy had stopped with a sudden fainting and fluttering at her heart. And now, while she turned her white, patient face toward the pulpit, strange fancies began to crowd her mind, interrupted only when Mr. Holworthy, in rounding off one of his turgid periods, brought out with extra force the beautiful words of St. Paul, " Love worketh no ill to his neighbour."

In Mrs. Holworthy's fancy, she seemed to see herself as she was at eighteen, a joyous care-free girl, with many tastes for art and books, and high companionships and charity, and great and noble deeds. Life, then, had stretched before her like a flower-

,strewn pathway, not devoid of suffering and sacrifice, to be sure, but the suffering and the sacrifice were to have had the sweetness and recompense of being her chosen own, freely accepted and joyfully submitted to with the sublime consciousness of her own soul's development thereby.

Then Mrs. Holworthy remembered with a sudden shudder in the retrospect, of her meeting with Mr. Holworthy. Did she love the heavy, phlegmatic young minister who visited at her father's house so long ago? No, she could see, oh, so clearly now, that she did not, that she had never known love, that she was too young and inexperienced to divine the depths of meaning in that word. She saw she had been somewhat flattered by the attentions of the young minister, that she had been drawn into marriage with him by the assiduous teaching that marriage was woman's sole sphere, and that marriage with a clergyman was eminently pure and respectable. As she looked back over her married life, she saw that at its very threshold she had been compelled to lay aside all her tastes for art, her aspirations for doing something good and noble in her own way, even her simple enjoyment of her own poor little life, all had been ruthlessly sacrificed. From the day that her first child was born, she had never known an unbroken night's rest, she had scarcely looked into a book, she had lost the use of her pen and pencil, the cares of breeding had absorbed her whole life, and what had she to show for them? Her children, to be sure; but even these could never compensate her for her ruthless · dispossession of all the golden opportunities and innocent cravings of her own nature.

As Mrs. Holworthy mused thus over her mutilated past, the beautiful text of Mr. Holworthy's sermon began to mingle with her thoughts, and to arouse strange questionings in her mind. Could these heathen " neighbours," whom Mr. Holworthy was seeking so strenuously in the far-off Isles of the Sea, have a more unmitigated slavery than hers had been? However unenlightened they might be, were they not quite as free and happy as she, bound as she had been to bear children for this great man, whether she wanted to or not, whether she was able to or not? Surely, if any one deserved pity and needed succour, it was one whose lot had been like hers. Her head began to feel strangely confused. She repeated Mr. Holworthy's text to herself, " Love worketh no ill to his neighbour." Beautiful words! What could they mean? It was plain that something had worked ill to her unreconciled life, and therefore it could not be love.

No, it was a blinding mistake, a fearful travesty, a hideous misnomer to call it love. "Love worketh no ill to his neighbour," she repeated till her brain was dizzy.

Just as the Rev. Mr. Holworthy had completed his great effort and driven the last nail home, as it were, by reciting for the last time the noble words of St. Paul which had formed the theme of his discourse, there was a sudden stir in the congregation. Mrs. Holworthy had fallen forward in her seat, and her children were peering at her face with the unsuspecting curiosity of those who have experienced neither care or sorrow. When the kind-hearted women who came to her relief had laid her on the cushioned seat, her lips moved as if she were repeating something, but the only word they could catch was "Love." She had gone to a place where love truly "worketh no ill to his neighbour."

"This is indeed a mysterious dispensation of Providence," said the Rev. Mr. Holworthy to his awe-stricken parishioners.

But the village doctor, who was a man of few words, confided to his wife that evening that he thought that Mrs. Holworthy had died of a "dispensation of children."

I had just finished reading this article in the *Bitter*

Cry, when there was a knock at my door, and Mr. Lister entered.

"Come Mr. Carford," he said, "it is past two o'clock and as the women's parade will not pass through this street, we must take our luncheon at once and go down to the public square."

I sprang up. "Let us go," I said. "I would not miss such a spectacle for worlds. The sun never looked down on its like before, and it probably never will again."

And taking a hasty luncheon, we left the house.

CHAPTER XII.

The street through which the women were to pass, was, we found when we reached it, already thickly lined with men, many of whom bore marks of their fearful struggle with fire of the night before. Arms and hands bound up in slings, and foreheads bandaged with cloths, told of the scathing wounds that had been received in the fiery conflict. Blanched and haggard faces and heavy eyes also told of sleepless anxiety before and after the fire. Some of those who had been so injured as to be unable to appear on the streets, were propped in easy chairs at the open windows. Not to see womankind after such an unprecedented absence, was a deprivation not to be endured. It would have been like missing the sight of the sun after a dreary, Arctic winter.

But though all the men in the town, excepting those who were disabled by wounds, were on the streets and squares through which the women were to pass, there was a silence like a spell upon the vast multitude. It was a perfectly noiseless congregation that had gathered there. Anything like gossip or badinage were as utterly absent as they would have been from before the altar of a cathedral. Truly there was no place for speech in that strange concourse, and Mr. Lister and I took our places in it without uttering a word. A feeling of solemnity akin to awe had taken possession of me. I recalled Mr. Lister's words when he first told me of the parade: " The women wish man to see in a simple panorama exactly what woman has been up to this day."

What could the panorama be?

But I did not have long to wait. And the tense excitement of the moment when the women appeared on the bridge, toward which all eyes were strained, how can I describe it! It seemed for a moment to make me dizzy. When the mist which swam before my eyes had cleared away, the head of a majestic host had crossed the bridge, and was slowly advancing, without noise or gesture, toward the spot where I stood.

Seen from a little distance, I remember a first vague impression that the women had taken great liberties with the fashions that had existed when I last saw them. I called to mind that Mr. Lister had told me that among the other relics of what had become to them an obsolete and withered past, the women had cast off many of the unreasoning fetters of fashion that they had spent much earnest study and practical experiment in their retirement in finding the most natural and comely dress for women. I will not say that the sight of women in any garb would not have been thrilling under such strange circumstances as those under which I was now about to behold her, but certainly the women who were approaching me were dressed with a simplicity and taste such as I had never before seen. Their comely outlines seemed invested with a new sense of freedom of motion such as one might have who had been suddenly released from a weary, dragging ball and chain.

But all thought of the vesture of these self-banished daughters of the Universe vanished like a breath the instant they drew near enough for me to note the rise and fall of their tremulous bosoms, to search their serious faces, and to study the arrangement of their noiseless and modest pageant. Their speechless procession was divided in a way that I did not at first comprehend, but there was a sense of plain, critical sincerity about it, a perception that it was intended to be a bare exposition of simple, unvarnished truth, that sharpened my intellect so that I was not long in perceiving its vivid meaning.

First in this strange procession came the unmarried women, or "old maids" as they had always been called, and although there were no upbraidings in their serious, modest eyes, the intolerable injustice and cruelty which had been meted out by man to these patient, helpless souls, was made as clear as the blackly vivid painting of a guilty conscience.

"These are they," a voice seemed to say, "whom man has for ages taunted with a derision as contemptible and unchivalrous as the striking of a cripple. These gentle sisters of men, who have been by their nature ever ready to perform the kindest and most sisterly acts for their recreant brothers, have been laughed to scorn if they manifested the slightest desire for marriage, and bitterly mocked if they failed. Spurred by contumely toward the only goal which man had allowed them, they had been heartlessly derided for missing it, and relegated to a life of coldness and contempt as cruel as the grave. Instead of reaching a strong, brotherly arm toward these sisters, man had added to her natural weakness the abuse of a coarse ridicule and the unutterably grievous burden of a cruel disrespect. To this had been added in innumerable instances, the single-

handed struggle with dire poverty." Before these
unreproaching creatures, who had suffered such un-
numerable cruelties at the hands of their natural
protectors, I felt a self-abasement that was akin to
remorse. I longed to throw myself in the dust before
them, to kiss their hands and to crave their forgiveness. Surely the woes of the " old maids " called
for the just vengeance of Heaven. And how many
there were of them! Who would have dreamed,
without seeing such a panorama as this, that so
large a proportion of women were old maids, living
in a state of contemptuous abasement or humiliating
sufferance? As I gazed at them, strange and confusing questions, never before thought of, began to
thrust themselves into my mind. Had not this
great mass of women social and maternal instincts as
deep and inexpugnable as any of their kind? What
sort of social system was this, then, that remorse-
lessly crushed and cruelly starved the strongest and
most innocent desires of a great majority of its
subjects? Could it be possible that sane men and
women believed that a just Heaven looked with any
complaisance upon such a system?

A space divided the old maids from the part of the
procession that came next, and I turned with curiosity to look at the faces of the men by whom I was

surrounded. To my satisfaction, I saw plainly written there the poignant workings of a deeply troubled conscience; I saw there the unutterable shame of having done an unchivalrous act, and the still heavier reproach of having done a cruel one. There was no need of upbraiding words.

The part of the procession which next drew near seemed to be nearly as numerous as the " old maids." With a sudden shock, I saw that it was the " courte-sans," or rather those who had been courtesans, for I remembered that Woman had, by an irrevocable edict, forever banished the name and calling of the courtesan from the earth.

But if the contemplation of the soul-wearying burdens borne by the uncomplaining " old maids " produced in the men who gazed upon them the com-punctions of pity and remorse, the scarred and wasted wrecks of man's passion which now passed in long review before him, reproached him with a piognancy ten-fold greater. These women, bearing the ineffaceable marks of man's ravages, had differed, it appeared, only by an accident from those whom he esteemed pure. Dragged from the garden of purity by man's own perfidy, they had been doomed without hope of forgiveness, to forever minister to is lust. Disregarding for ages the example and spirit of the Great Teacher, man had thrust the victims he had thus made, deeper and deeper into the blackness of a bottomless pit. I turned away my head with a shudder from a spectacle before which all men stood in awful condemnation!

Fully two-thirds of the procession had passed by, and the woman's panorama had shown nothing but unmerited contumely or ruthless devastation. What could there be left?

It was a band of exceedingly frail and wasted women, that I next looked upon. Feeble invalids they appeared with but a remnant of days before them. Borne down by disease they dragged out lives of continual pain. The ashes of hope were in their eyes, the ashes of beauty were in their faces, and the ashes of strength were in their feeble frames. These, it appeared, were women who had married young profligates, "to save them." They looked like flowers which had been hopelessly blasted by a deadly, blighting wind. The fearful scars and moral pollution which had been in the souls of their husbands, had been wrecked upon them to the uttermost, and there had been no voice to protest, no sheltering arm to interpose.

These were followed by a very small band of women who were said to have been happily married. But the chains-of these seemed in many respects as heavy, though a little more gilded, than those of the women who had preceded them. They appeared to have paid their all for the narrow happiness which they enjoyed, and it had been fraught with deadly perils, against which they had had no adequate protection. Even some of these, it seemed, had been bartered for gold or titles, and only a filmy legal fiction stood between them and the name and stain of the concu- bine. Following them closely was the army of married women, who, unfortunately mismated or overborne by the evils of undesired maternity and its dire accompaniment, poverty, formed the strong rank and file of the Great Woman's Strike.

As I gazed upon them, a strange hallucination possessed me. It seemed to me that I was looking, not merely at the passing procession, but at the tender mothers of all mankind, and that, with them, I saw the mountain of anguish, the unremembered toil, the care and undying self-sacrifice which they had borne since the race began. What did not man owe to woman!

In the close of the procession came the young women who were just verging upon marriageable age, the tender and blooming maidens who were still dallying in the primrose path of free and beautiful girlhood. The sight of these innocent and care-free creatures would seem to have lightened and dissipated the effect of the sight of the unabated misery that had preceded them, but on the contrary, it immeasurably heightened the awful effect. For these, it appeared, were the perfumed and garlanded victims who were soon to be offered up to the fearful Moloch who presided over woman's destiny. "A few short years," it seemed to say, "and the rosy hours of youth's unfettered dance will be over. Then, I claim you for the three great classes into which women are divided,—despised old maids, feeding on the social crusts thrown from a profligate's table; equally despised courtesans, sitting at that table with man in wanton revelry; and married menials, propagative drudges, meekly waiting upon that table, having no voice in the allotment of their own destiny, and no power over their own persons."

This voice ringing in my ears, together with the woeful procession which had passed before my eyes, had completely daunted me. I could bear it no longer. It was as if my conscience had been preternaturally aroused, and had brought before my mind's eye, in long defile, a black array of unsuspected sins. Rapt as I had been in the contemplation of this strange procession, I felt that I must flee from it as I would flee from a spot where I had committed a dastardly crime. I turned in anguish to break my way through the crowd of men, anywhere to get away from the awful evidence of misery in the producing of which I had been an accomplice with all men. Judge, then, of my speechless amazement, my absolute horror, on turning, to find that there was not a man in sight. Pierced as I had been with an agonising contrition, it still appeared that I was more callous than the men by whom I had been surrounded. Unable to bear the heavy reproach of their consciences, they had slunk away one after another, till I, without knowing it, had been left entirely alone. This discovery was too great for my nerves, weakened as they had been by the ceaseless shocks of the past few days. My brain whirled. I was conscious of a sudden movement toward me by some of the women in the procession and then all was a blank.

I had fainted.

CHAPTER XIII.

I did not remain unconscious long. When I revived, I was lying on some wraps which were spread upon the ground near where I had stood, and gentle hands were bathing my forehead. I opened my eyes, and saw that two women were kneeling over me with solicitous faces, while a third, a commanding brunette, stood a little way off watching us. The rest of the procession were returning across the bridge toward the women's home.

The first thought that came into my mind as I opened my eyes and saw the gentle faces hovering over me, was that henceforth I should love all women, that as a sex they were forever entitled to the deep and admiring admiration and affection of all men. Until a new and more humane social order should be safely established, I would patiently bide my time without license or anarchy, but no power on earth should prevent me from loyally regarding every woman as my sister from that time forth. I murmured confused thanks for their kindness, and arose in deep embarrassment.

"Are you well enough to go to your home?" said the young woman who had been watching us. Her manner was that of sincere solicitude, unmixed with either embarrassment or affectation.

"Yes, thank you," I said, and turned briskly on my heel; but I had gone but a few steps when my feet began to falter; my knees were strangely weak.

"I think you had better see him safely home," said the brunette to the two women under whose ministrations I had revived. Weak as I was I could not refuse, and the two women, gently taking each an arm, began to slowly walk with me toward Mr. Lister's house.

Many times during the past few days, as the reader knows, it had seemed to me that I must be dreaming, such was the astounding strangeness of my surroundings. Let him then imagine what a wildly preposterous vision it must have seemed to me, Rodney Carford, to be escorted by two women toward a home in a town in which woman had utterly forsaken man. To be thus escorted, too, on the eve of the casting of a ballot which was to decide the perpetuity of the human race!

*T*o add to the overpowering strangeness of my situation, I suddenly realized that the two women who were accompanying me toward Mr. Lister's home belonged to the two most injured classes in the women's panorama. One was an old maid, and the other had been a courtesan. *T*his discovery revived in my mind the deep remorse which I had felt in beholding their pathetic pageant. I remember weakly trying to decide in my mind which of the two had been most cruelly injured by man. I longed to throw my arms around them both, but I scarcely dared to look into their faces as we walked slowly along. At last, as I stood at the door of Mr. Lister's house, I raised my eyes to theirs. " Forgive me," I said to the old maid. " Forgive me," I said to the courtesan. They made no reply, but a serene light, unmixed with any bitterness, shone in their eyes and gave me comfort. As they turned away after leaving me at the door of Mr. Lister's house, I followed them wistfully with my eyes. They had wound their arms about each other like sisters, and without a single backward glance, were walking toward the bridge.

I have no recollection how I passed the night that ensued, but I suppose I must have slept. I remember that Mr. Lister had retired when I entered the house, and as I felt no inclination for conversation, it was a relief to me to seek the solitude of my room.

The day on which the ballots were to be cast dawned as all other days of great import to the human days have dawned. Although it was a day that was to decide a question never before conceived of, and one that involved the possible extinction of the human race, it was not marked by any demonstration of any kind. On the contrary, the conspicuous thing about the day, making it totally unlike any previous balloting in the world's history, was the noiselessness with which everything was conducted. There were no harangues upon the street corners, no attempt at persuasion anywhere, not even any inquiry among men as to how individuals were going to vote. Each man seemed wholly wrapped in his own thoughts, but there was a stern directness of manner, a total absence of any appearance of vacillation, that showed that the time for the decision was ripe.

The system of voting was the Australian, and how each man was to vote was a secret known only to his own soul. After spending some time with Mr. Lister in visiting the polling-places, I returned to the house to pass the day as best I could in his library.

At noon Mr. Lister returned with an interesting

piece of news.   The polls were to close at four o'clock, and at that hour the women were to assemble in the great Auditorium which formed one of the group of buildings which they occupied.   There they were to await the report of the decision of the ballots, and any one was free to go there to hear it.   To pass the time till then I reminded Mr. Lister of his promise to give me " Zugassent's Discovery."   He placed the book in my hands, and, having arranged with me to meet him at the Woman's Auditorium at four o'clock, he left the house to attend to business per-taining to the balloting.

It was with a feeling of rare curiosity, not unmixed with profound awe, that I opened a book which promised to have made a discovery of value in a field in which no other discoverer had ever had the temerity to set foot.   That this discovery was as innocent of evil as the white light of day, and pro-foundly scientific as well, that it was in keeping with the noble advancement of man in all other depart-ments of wisdom, I was assured both from what I had been told of the character of Zugassent, and because it commended itself to such pure-minded. lovers as Justin Lister and Allegra Alliston.   But I had not the slightest idea of what this discovery might be. . I accordingly plunged into the book as one plunges on a summer's day in a stream of whose depth he has no conception.

As I got deeper and deeper into "Zugassent's Discovery," my interest became absorbingly, wonderfully, and overpoweringly intense. I forgot all about the Great Woman's Strike. I forgot where I was. I forgot everything which had happened in the exciting days through which I had just passed. Hour after hour flew by, and as I turned page after page there was gradually unfolded to my wondering perceptions a discovery that appeared to be the perfection of chivalry, the essense of unselfishness, the culminating and consummate flower of the true refinement of all ages. Civilizing and ennobling man beyond all precedent, it seemed to lift the primeval curse from woman not less really than if it had been done by an Omnipotent fiat. With breathless interest I read on. Once only I paused, as the question rose in my mind, " Was it feasible?" At that critical moment a clock struck, and I counted the strokes. Five o'clock! Like a flash the recollection of everything came back to me. It was an hour after the time at which I had promised to meet Mr. Lister at the Woman's Auditorium! Thrusting " Zaugassent's Discovery " into my pocket, I seized my hat, and leaving the house, hurried toward the bridge which led to the women's home.

CHAPTER XIV.

As I entered the Auditorium, and hastened to a seat beside Mr. Lister, I saw that the vast floor was filled with men and women, but that they were separated by a wide space. A woman whom I quickly recognized as Allegra Alliston was speaking from the platform. As I entered she was saying;

"Remove but this monstrous shadow which continually yawns over woman's life, and she promises to become the true glory of man, and to cheer and lighten his pathway with a radiance more dazzling than his wildest dreams ever conceived of."

As the speaker proceeded I became conscious that I was surrounded by a growing tumult of weeping. The deep conviction of having cruelly oppressed and wronged and ravaged woman for unnumbered ages, which I had seen on the strained and anxious faces of the men when I first entered the hall, had given way to sobs and groans. The speaker paused for a moment with emotion. Suddenly as if it had been traced by a hand on the wall, the conviction burst upon that weeping multitude that immeasurably above all ties of consanguity, and even higher than any more sentimental tie, clear and serene stood the great, practical truth that all men and women were brothers and sisters, the children of one common Father, and as such were forever entitled to each other's deepest love and compassion. Filled with this sublime thought, they gazed at each other with the glistening, eager eyes that welcome a long absent brother or sister.

The speaker seemed inspired with this thought. With a radiant smile, she continued :

" You weep at the contemplation of the bitter woes of the past. Let me, I beseech you, lift up your eyes to the near glories of a possible future, when the new man and woman, neither oppressing nor oppressed, shall pass down the centuries hand in hand ministering to each other from the sweet fountains of eternal affection. Who shall say that in that union a power may not be evolved from which Death himself shall draw back dismayed ?"

As the speaker concluded, she did not perceive that a dainty little girl had entered the building unnoticed, and come upon the stage. In one hand she bore a white rose, and in the other a paper to which she sought to draw the speaker's attention by tugging at her garments. There was a murmur among the audience that it was the news of the decision of the ballots, the guarantee on which the the fate of not only a single race but all races hung.

Miss Alliston caught the deep significance of the murmur. She took the paper in her trembling hands, and pressing it against her tumultuous bosom, advanced to the front of the platform. Instantly every man in the great building arose, and with eyes rivetted intently on the paper, waited as if for a sentence of doom or a joyful pardon.

The fearful suspense of that crucial moment! How can I describe it? It seemed as if the very atmosphere of the room throbbed with so high a magnetic tension that it must burst. A deathly stillness had succeeded the storm of weeping. Pale as marble and with one pleading glance at the foremost row of stern, but wan-faced men, Allegra Alliston opened the paper. For a time, which seemed agonizing ages, her eyes rested on the contents. Then her hand containing the paper slowly dropped to her side. A seraphic smile beamed upon her countenance, as she said, in a voice broken with emotion:

" The shadow is removed from woman. The guarantee is granted forev———."

But the reaction of the pent-up emotion of that awful alienation could be stayed no longer. It seemed as though nothing in Heaven above or on the earth beneath could restrain what followed. With a cry which must have been heard at the throne of God, and before Allegra Alliston could finish her sentence, the men and women in that vast hall had rushed into each other's arms as the uncontrollable sea rushes back to its pristine bed. There were tears, but they were tears of such illimitable joy as earth had never seen before, and might never see again. Homely or handsome, it mattered not. In that souls' jubilee there was a brother's and a sister's joyful caress for every one.

It seemed as though my heart must burst at beholding the mighty spectacle of man and woman thus forever reconciled and united as they never had been since they were driven from the Garden of Eden. In the vehemence of my emotions, I essayed to rise, to speak, to cry out I know not what; but, instead, I awoke from what had been but a dream. I was sobbing with convulsive joy.

FINIS.

opular Edition
Bellamy Library

ONE SHILLING
(*Cloth 2/-*).

THE

O-OPERATIVE

COMMONWEALTH

AN

POSITION OF MODERN SOCIALISM

BY

L. GRONLUND

Edited by GEORGE BERNARD SHAW

CPSIA information can be obtained
at www.ICGtesting.com
Printed in the USA
LVOW01s1000260317

528497LV00027B/551/P